The Long Island Horror

A Modern Novel

Richard A. Boehler, Jr.

authorHOUSE®

AuthorHouse™
1663 Liberty Drive
Bloomington, IN 47403
www.authorhouse.com
Phone: 833-262-8899

Published by AuthorHouse 09/16/2022

ISBN: 978-1-6655-7049-7 (sc)
ISBN: 978-1-6655-7048-0 (e)

Contents

"*Fiction is the truth located inside the center of a communities lies*" (S.K.).

"*The story presented in this manuscript is purely fictional, or is it?*" (R.B.).

Acknowledgements:

1. **The music.** To all the band directors, at all levels of education = for leadership, guidance and experience in the "wind ensembles". Concerts were amazing and marching bands were a challenge (e.g., choreography during marching band competitions). The band members always worked hard to learn the music. The friendships and love are forever embedded in memories.

2. **The football team and weight room.** To all the coaches, at all levels of sports = for leadership, guidance and the

experience of "discipline" and "teamwork". Every sore ankle, broken bone, dislocated shoulder, bump and bruise was worth it.

3. **The United States Military.** For the topnotch, unique training of this great nation: The United States of America. All heart and soul. "Honor, Courage and Commitment". Need I say more.

4. **To the University.** For the breath of knowledge and depth of wisdom shared through various academic curriculum. The challenges were many and the experiences gained offered a path to "higher level thinking", which is essential in this world. To the dedicated professors, assistants and all levels of staff: the diligent efforts really made a difference in students lives.

Late night labs to learn the blood flow through chambers of the human heart, dissections of dog sharks, titrations with chemicals and a variety of unique laboratory techniques taught students the "way of science" (i.e., the scientific method). And all this is carried with each student throughout life.

5. **To all the great writers**. I always enjoyed Michael Crichton and Stephenie Meyer. Especially, Stephen King (S.K.), for leadership and the many samples of what it means to be a good writer. Specifically, the guidance of S.K. impacted me in the following way: (paraphrasing) = write a lot and read a lot. Write, even if it amounts to nothing more than a pile of **IT. Keep writing. And that inspired me to at least

give it a go, utilize what I know and reach deep inside to be creative. My whole life has admired such creative leaders like S.K.. The creativity is wonderful in this life, and it is also seen in great art, heard in innovative music, displayed in unique characters of movies and created in innovative science.

6. **To wisdom.** For teaching a wild child the true meaning of being humble. In teaching that a rough boy could in fact grow to be a person "they never thought he could be" = "a gentleman" (although, always part wolf).

7. **To the mystery of "Faith".**

Chapter 1

There was a uniqueness about "Long Island". Perhaps it had to do with the location of the island or maybe it was the established culture. The place had some history, but seemed to hide most of the secrets very well. That is until a clear pattern of "accidents", "sickness" and unsolved murders were detected. Not only were the patterns being detected, but a survivor of attempted murder caught the attention of a high order.

There were many good people on Long Island. These were the type of people that were the best "unsuspecting victims" to such grotesque schemes, plots, plans of horror. The good souls of Long Island went about their business each week, each month – with goals to own a home, to get married, go to school, serve some time with uncle Sam, enjoy the beaches – that were some goals for most good people; in no particular chronological order.

The northeast region of the United States was a nice area to raise a family. There were four very well-defined seasons that most people enjoyed. And even if one season was not so enjoyable, the next season always approached pretty quickly. The area wasn't nice just because of the north east U.S. region though. Long Island was essentially an island, surrounded by the Atlantic-ocean and some bays with protective barrier regions of land. Being surrounded with ocean kept the local climate somewhat mild.

The farms that remained over the years, were located further east on the island. The eastern part of Long Island was located about half way out from the NY city life, a short one-hour drive east of Manhattan and Sunnyside Queens. Traveling away from the city area was a relaxing experience, with lots of scenery to see. The suburban neighborhoods were very unique to Long Island. They were filled with local pride, parades, junior and high school traditions (for example pep rally football games).

The Mitchel field area still housed many military operations for Marine Corps and Navy, including the local commissary and exchange. Great areas to buy some food for the home. A small airport, "Republic" also housed many military jets for quick trips to many local and not so local military bases. The pilots of routine training exercises in amazing jets always welcomed some buddies to accompany their quick travel to Virginia, Florida, Rhode Island and California. Off the grid stuff, of course.

Farms and wineries were popular attractions for tourists and the local residents. Depending on the season, the farms were ready for a variety of visitors that were eager to go apple picking, pumpkin picking or just enjoy a peaceful stroll on a weekend. Sometimes in life there is no rational explanation. The events are so sinister, so evil that a rational person can be driven into a state of psychological breakdown, just trying to make sense of it all. He was lucky to survive. Every day is a gift, that was for sure. So much had happened, where to start?

Prior to the entrance of "evil"

This is not a "little house on the prairie" story. No, this is a story with psychological thrills. It takes place in the northeast region of the United States of America and involves two kids born into a living, breathing circle of hell. Not to different from "Dante's Inferno". With one exception, the evil is very real and alive, with ground zero in suburbia, Long Island. So, if the events are odd, are bizarre, are not understandable at times – keep up, it's a psychological mess that has its origins 40 to 50 years before these two kids were even born into it.

The kids are of high school age, perhaps one could call them young adults. Their names are Gina and Randy. Prior to meeting in band camp, they lived mere minutes from each other. The high school years were…. "interesting". Aren't most high school years curiously interesting? For these two, the years were "special". A lot was shared, and Randy was thankful for that "place and time". Sort of a "protective barrier" to what was happening in the local town of Patchogue-Medford. Coming from this type of environment, kids (the unguided ones) look to "light" for the opportunity to "survive". Randy had little guidance, in fact it pretty much was a "free-for all/zoo" with much danger. For example, stupid situations were common to Randy.

The beaches of long Island were awesome to visit. However, during hurricane season (late summer) the beaches could be treacherous. Having little guidance in this type of environment can sometimes set the stage for tragedy. A trip to the beach when a hurricane is just south of Long Island is a "stupid idea" for anyone. But, there we were – high school kids on the beach where waves (huge waves) were breaking at the base of where the large life guard stands were located. Could you imagine the crest of this type of ocean wave? Its big! The beach was about to be closed. It was just dangerous.

Two fit guys, standing at the shore, were about to jump into the turbulent/treacherous waters. Problem was that the waves were so damn big, it was almost impossible to find the right time to enter the ocean. Randy and his buddy had planned to count to five, then enter the ocean. One, two… and after five, Randy was in the treacherous ocean waters – looking toward the shore at his friend who did not jump in! That view did not last long, the waves were enormous and cresting from every direction (horizontal hits and vertical hits). The undertow immediately started sucking him further out to sea. Time passed and muscles weakened. The human body has strength, he was a good swimmer…. After what seemed to be at least an hour the last wave crashed into him, from the blindside and he went under. This last hit from the treacherous water brought him under where at this point placing his arm up toward the sky did not reach any "air". There was only water. It was over for this stupid kid.

Then his eyes opened as he lay on his back in the wet shore sand – with a life guard standing over him. The ocean wave spat this body onto the shore and the life guard had sprinted over to see if he was alive. Dazed, but coherent – Randy lived…. They say hind site is "20/20". This was the first divine intervention that occurred, or was it just coincidence….

It was "puppy love", "young love" – perhaps…. Maybe a little more. It was a union between two souls in such a cruel place. Something special, although there was immaturity – she loved him, she took care of his wounds (both physical and emotional).

Young men don't have much restraint when it comes to emotion. Especially a 185 pound punk that worked hard to develop a 400-pound squat and 275 to 315 pound bench press in the local gym weight room. He loved her to, he protected her. They were a couple growing closer together and learning that although life was not perfect, they did have each other.

It seemed that some young men (and perhaps even men that are more developed) are just disrespectful; it is in their nature. Randy did not like this. It could be that it was the immaturity, the lack of experience, or maybe just a sense of jealousy. Randy surely had elevated levels of testosterone from ingestion of amino acids, lifting of heavy weights… proliferation of the musculature with this sort of developmental path, sometimes leads to overly aggressive situations. Or maybe he was just protective of his love.

Most of the time Randy was a genuinely calm and reserved force. It was the surroundings though, an evil place with clear evil. He sensed the evil, often, to often (it was a gift, or a curse, depending on how one looked at it). I guess Randy could be perceived as a bully type. But not for the general public, only a bully against EVIL - which really wasn't such a bad thing, was it?

The boom of the "practical computer", with internet capability was new during this point in time. In fact, even though the practical computer was being utilized by the general public – the word processor was more familiar. Since there was more familiarity with the word processor, most people would type enormous essays, reports on this "super type writer". And the documents would be saved onto a floppy or hard disk. This was just as cool as the tape deck; which was still being used to compile "mixed tapes" of favorite music.

Gina left, got far away from the circle of hell; Long Island. She travelled to bridgewater (a college in Virginia) to study biology. Randy stayed local, commuted to the University on Long Island. But often left the circle of hell to travel on military flights to where-ever the orders directed him to. Quick flights to Virginia to catch a Naval ship was the first military command attachment/support destination. The University classes made use of the "internet", "the practical computer". Countless hours were spent in science libraries studying, digesting, and re-studying. The competition was fierce and a massive number of students enrolled, did not make the cut, then left. It was intimidating at times, and other times it was invigorating – a refreshing sense of accomplishment after all the hard work was put in to University studies.

Once or twice a week, Randy traveled to the chemistry or physics libraries to log into the "practical internet/computer". "Email" was something new! And he often communicated with Gina. How cool. To communicate, continue letters to one another while they were in two very different States (Virginia and Long Island NY). Even though the "circle of hell" existed, there were a few areas of "light", angelic – sent and/or built from the heavens to help good souls survive.

That light was (A) the long island beaches, (B) the University campus community and (C) the military base in Amityville, NY.

Yes, they say hindsight is 20/20. During holidays Gina would meet Randy at the University. Looking back at it/reflecting – it seemed she might have been reaching out to build/re-build more than just a friendship. Randy enjoyed her company. She was a special soul. And he was happy that she was in a school that was far away from the circle of hell on Long Island. They were close friends and he sensed she was looking for more than just the friendship they had. Randy drove a nice black pick up truck, and one afternoon Gina was a passenger in the vehicle. They were listening to "my immortal", which is a very emotional song with heart-felt lyrics. As the song played in the car, Randy drove and Gina gently placed her hand on his leg. They looked at each other and she began to sing the lyrics of the song. She was reaching for him. Randy felt it and wanted to believe that he could go down that path, again. But, he could not. Sadly, an intense feeling of "betrayal" and "sadness" filled his mind. He enjoyed their friendship and he was thankful for all the love, over the years. But, he would always only be a "good friend to her". Randy was a "rational type of guy". So, even though he knew this in his heart – he did also believe that sometimes divine intervention would create miracles. Perhaps he thought, somewhere deep in his mind, that there could be a place and time they would reunite…. If that was even possible? Whatever the case was one thing was for sure, Gina's love had saved him from destruction as he survived in this circle of Hell, Long Island.

The University was built on a nice patch of Long Island property, in the north most region – overlooking the water. The stretch of water between Long Island and Connecticut was "the Long Island Sound". A calm bay-like area that was typically less turbulent than the surrounding Atlantic Ocean. Research buildings were observed throughout various parts of the land. Surrounding the University was also a thick body of forest. Research for the environmental biologists were plentiful in these woods. Randy had met a brilliant Russian lady during this time. She was fashion savvy, loved to wear long stiletto shoes, leopard skirts and Hollywood style sun glasses. Her hair was golden blond that reached below her hips. Yeah, her style turned a lot of glances her way – her style went well with her long athletic legs. Randy and Ivanka shared an interest in technology, innovation and all the challenges that surrounded that path. The classes were extremely challenging, competitive and most did not make it to the end of the semester. Average class sizes began with 1000 students and ended with 100 to 200. Not to stressful, yeah sure. Anyway, through each immense (what seemed to be unattainable) process struggle to learn the required curriculum, they were together. Randy admired her brilliance. It was quite amazing actually. He never met a lady so pretty and incredibly bright. He prided himself with pretty good intellectual ability, but after studying with her many evenings, it was clear that she was a super star!

The students at University were studying to become doctors, biologists, professors, medical gurus in various areas (occupational therapy, sports medicine), teachers, nurses, sociologists, psychologists, mathematicians, physicists and more – super science people. Students came from all over the world: United States, Russia, China, Japan, India, and other places. It was an incredible melting pot of competition. The concepts were tough enough, but Randy and Ivanka also valued the study of "music". They studied early classical music together (Baroque, Beethoven, Mozart). One evening they stumbled upon a secret research experiment being performed in the basement of the physics building. "ROYGBIV", the colors of the rainbow (red, orange, yellow, green, blue, indigo, violet) were shining from a doorway propped open, in an experiment lab.

The project lead came out after the experiment was complete. His name was Michael. What did you guys see? Randy and Ivanka just said "light", colorful light. What were you studying tonight? The experiment mixed a variety of technical concepts that basically revealed the capabilities of "anti-matter". Anti-matter has the ability to open a "black hole" in time/space. And when directed accurately/precisely, the process can be utilized to transport objects and people from one area to the next. The problem with this experiment was that Michael was evil, with too many ties to an evil community – Long Island. Randy and Ivanka left the physics building that night, intrigued and frightened by the lack of moral fibers in Michael. What was he using the black hole experiment for? Where did the experiment transport things to?

Anti-matter, when formulated perfectly has the ability to open up a space in time. The current understanding was not available. In fact, most regulatory bodies banned extensive research with anti-matter since there was a concern of "what a black hole was". Earth based telescopes have peered into the horizon of distant outer space black holes. On planet Earth, the three biggest telescopes were located in three different regions: South America, North America and in Antarctica. The astronomers linked each telescope to focus on outer space black holes, in order to gain insight/a better understanding of the inner working of this "anti-matter". To date, there was too much uncertainty. But, the astronomers knew this: light travelling from the brightest outer-space star could not escape the black hole. Everything, including light that travelled even near the black hole was sucked into it. Nothing escaped the gravity of the black hole. But, where was the light disappearing to? Objects like space rock also disappeared. Where did these space rocks disappear to? The theory was that as light approached the anti-matter (the black-hole), it entered a "rip in time" and it travelled to another place (perhaps another time). Albert Einstein theorized "worm holes" in outer space, that could transport to other galaxies. Physics was a tough subject to digest at times.

There were practical applications. For example: studying physics at University breathed life into the natural light. The spectrum of light, visible and invisible light. ROYGBIV, the colors of the rainbow were there and were visible as red, orange, yellow, green, blue, indigo and violet. The workings of an engine, the workings of a home refrigerator: thermal dynamics…. Pretty cool knowledge, lots of mathematical formulas and theory…. but, very practical applications in real life. Not all physics was so practical though (at least, not practical in terms of real day to day life). Einstein wrote about time travel in space. Tough challenges to any student sitting in a mid-term exam: twin A and twin B are studied. Twin A, age 20 stays on Earth as twin B leaves on a space ship into deep space for 20 years. When twin B returns from the space trip: how old is twin A and how old is twin B? There was a theoretical formula that Einstein created; amazing stuff that was hard to understand.

Michael had an in-depth understanding of the Einstein formulas and practical application of such formulas in the lab. What was he using the formulas to create? Some sort of anti-matter/black hole transport experiment? Transport to where? And why? Was this anti-matter stable? Was it even safe for Michael, his assistant and for the University? Or maybe there should have been a concern for the safety of the "Earth". Theories and observations in space showed that nothing escaped the gravity of anti-matter/black holes. What if someone created a black hole on Earth? Wouldn't that sort of experiment suck in and destroy all people and objects that were near it?

It was a quite evening after that. Studying genetics with Ivanka was always a treat. How was it possible that such brilliance could exist in one mind? She was impressive. Even brilliant souls need a rest. They closed the books and actually quickly moved the books from the bed to the floor as they gently caressed one another…. After-wards she insisted that he not turn around until she was dressed. Of course, Randy being the rebel wondered why and turned around – she giggled and said "I told you to stay turned around"! very cute; he thought that it must have been a Russian cultural thing?

The black hole experiment continued, in secret as the semester progressed. The experiment was perfected by the end of winter semester. Why would anyone want to work with such volatile materials? Randy read that the anti-matter had some very bad consequences, if not handled properly. Evil rarely operates alone; mostly because it is weak. Sadly, the forces of evil operate in a sick spiral of a network. In many ways, the spiral network is quicker than the computer internet. Yes, evil operates in a network. And that was certainly the case on Long Island. No one ever imagined though that the network travelled with lightning speed to another part of the world. The network travelled via a controlled experiment that was operating off the north fork coast of Long Island: once called "plum island", but now desolate (owned by the government). The small island was a quick ferry ride from the northeast shore of Long Island. However, the island had been abandoned for the past fifty or so years.

The towns of Long Island were populated with many great people. Men and women with good souls. Their goals were aligned with "the American dream". Raise a family, enjoy life, live-laugh and love as much as possible. The unsuspecting "victims" of the hidden evil had no idea how deep the roots grew over the years. Living on Long Island, it was obvious and very difficult to ignore some of the "red flags". For example, the murders that occurred from time to time, happened with the oddest of circumstances. The people that were investigating, the news reporters that were presenting, the doctors that analyzed — they all had a part in the evil network.

Randy recalled his friend who had been married to one of the evil residents of Long Island. She and her network called themselves "women". They were not. Soulless entities that used and used to obtain property, money and what ever else they desired. These soulless entities used sex as a weapon. The news never presented much truth that surrounded the inner workings of this part of the evil network. Any type of sex, any desire was a savage tool that these evil "women" used. And when they were done – some would poison their mates (similar to the "black widow" spider). Randy had a friend that mysteriously entered a hospital after abrupt illness. He suspected that his wife had poisoned his morning coffee.

During his stay at the local Long Island hospital he was visited by his wife's family. He recalled the smug look of guilt on their faces, almost a sense of happiness that he had been hospitalized. Later in the week he was visited by his wife and he recalled the oddest statement by her to Randy's friend: "watch the nurse, don't take any pills from her – she is crazy, she might give you something to hurt you". Jake (Randy's friend) was so exhausted after being poisoned that he did not say much. He just sensed such an enormous presence of evil; then went back to sleep…. God knows how long he slept?

His friend doesn't recall much during his sleep. However, there were some defining moments that he was reluctant to talk about. Mostly because people would not understand his vision (including his own understanding of the vision). The darkness was peaceful, calm, quiet – with an enormous source of power. Immense, like the power of a raging ocean; just in the form of a quiet environment. Jakes friend was an elite warrior that lost his life in the mountains of Afghanistan, to savages with no regard for human life. The elite in the Navy are called "frog men" (Navy Seals). Best of the best, able to travel through the harshest conditions on land sea and air (including the mountains). Some argued that the mountains of Afghanistan were a stretch for the SEAL capabilities – Jake didn't think so. Jakes friend was also savage (when called upon to be savage, in the name of "protection" against rogue world savages).

They say after you leave this earth, you travel a bit (in human earth time, it could be years; 5 to 10). Randy's friend crossed over (after life) in approximately the year 2011; his warrior friend perished honorably in war, on Earth in the year 2005. Crossing over is not immediate. There is an enormous raging river (immense, similar to the Mississippi river, perhaps even bigger). Randy's friend Jake was floating in the river, in a strong current toward —— the end (most likely where you go at the very end….), when he was pulled out of the river by a strong arm of a warrior, gently placing Jake onto the shore, located next to the river. The vision was all peaceful, with little color – actually just about all gray in view. Exhausted from the travel, Jake looked up to thank his friend for rescuing him from the peaceful river. His friend was not there; he spotted him in the distance on what looked like a mountain – busy and focused on a piece of military communications equipment. Jake had no strength to yell or no real way to get his attention. Shortly after this vision, Jake woke in the hospital room… Randy's friend Jake was one of many victim's of the Long Island evil. Many of the victims were severely sickened, maimed and most just died an odd agonizing, puzzling death.

It's hard to pinpoint the exact time when "evil entered". Perhaps the evil was always there, but hidden – a secret, that was hidden from the unsuspecting victim. Perhaps the evil took hold of a good soul (he wanted to believe that). It's just that Randy recalled this evil entity named "Margo", had an enormous amount of hate in her heart. Not just hate, it was more than hate – it represented a legion of hate that was deep rooted in Long Island; a culture that consisted of many, many that co-evolved with criminals over a long period of time. There were times that Margo would say "she is DEAD to me" or "he is DEAD to me". It's not what was said. People say stupid things when they are mad. No, it is not what was said, many times. It was "how it was said".

Scary shit…. She meant it; the way she said it. It was almost like she had murdered prior to meeting him or that she was privy to murders of unsuspecting innocent victims that did not survive the wrath of this evil entity. The Long Island community sadly had many "Margo's" in it. These soulless men and soulless women owned homes, volunteered in town ambulance companies and had a very deep network of evil.

The Patchogue, Long Island Contact

Most people were good, and most people in the small-town community of Patchogue had a goal to live, love and laugh as much as possible – living the American Dream. Raising a family, visiting the wonderful Long Island beaches, enjoying the various restaurants and making memories along the way. Randy wanted to believe that, he wanted to believe that most people were good. But, this community had routes of evil. The community had a route population of "people" that operated in a mafiosa fashion. They were not mafia, they were just pure evil. Even the mafia had a respect for heaven, for church, for Jesus and Mary. However, pure evil has an effective way of blending into the community, blending in by hiding in the local churches, hiding in the school system, hiding and thriving in local volunteer organization (e.g., in Ambulance companies).

The evil flourished in the Patchogue community. These people owned homes, owned businesses, had dirt on local doctors, had dirt on local school officials. It was the so-called women (they were not women, just soulless entities with women parts) and the men (they were not men, they were cowards, supporters of criminals and in fact criminals) that were especially able to obtain the "dirt on various businesses". The women used "sex" as a weapon and when backed into a corner, they used the sex to target the good in the community. They knew the local and regional laws and were very sinister in the approach to targeting unsuspecting men. It was very easy to get a man in jail when the evil entity cried "he sexually assaulted me".

The evil was saturated in the community, most good people went about their daily lives and tried to ignore it. However, inside they were in a state of fear because they knew that the local news broadcasters were part of the evil. They also knew that the local doctors and schools and businesses were routed in this evil. It was evil because when crossing the path of evil…. evil murdered. These "people" were "soulless". The opposition was murdered; simple as that. If any perceived opposition was felt by the evil, in any way…. The opposition was targeted and murdered. The Long Island community was a circle of hell, not too different from the circles of hell presented in "Dante's Inferno". The poet Dante fell asleep in the 1300s and dreams of a travel through the depths of hell, and through purgatory and eventually into heaven. One has to wonder if it was more than a dream, more than a vision. Perhaps part of the vision was just the reality that Dante observed the circles of hell on Earth. The circle of Hell that was similar to the Long Island Community. What was even more evil (if that was possible), was that the evil was supported by the local news to cover it all up. Immediately after a murder the local news would start spinning the story. The local newspapers would start printing articles that implemented a psychological approach termed "projection". The evil community worked in sync and projected itself on the good. But where were the murdered bodies disappearing to? The bodies that were not able to be covered up well with the evil organizations. For example: it was pretty simple for the evil "soulless women," to claim that it was just a heart attack or an attack by a homeless person. This was simple because these evil soulless women co-evolved with homeless people, they co-evolved with criminals and they had a network of high level school officials that were targeted with "sexual weapons" (good way to black mail and cover up most murders). Blame the murders on a homeless person, blame the murders on a criminal; but at the route of the murders were the people that lived and owned houses in the community! There was also plenty of cash to fuel this sinister cover up, since the evil had collected insurance money over many years after unsuspecting victim husbands were mysteriously taken out/murdered.

But it wasn't just the soulless women. Basically, it was soulless people. Randy's friend Gina was in a relationship with a real shit head. A coward of a human being (and that is being nice). Insecure in his manhood, he abused Gina psychologically. She was not allowed to have much contact with friends, especially with Randy. But, she sneaked telephone calls to her friend. Mainly just to say hi, but since they were aware of the evil and she, sadly, was growing more aware of the evil in her current relationship – she wanted to make sure Randy was still alive. Every conversation started the same with her = "hey, how are you?", Gina would then follow with the question/statement "are you ok? Just wanted to make sure you still were alive". Hindsight is 2020, and Randy realized that she was trying to warn him that her boyfriend was evil, she was trapped in it (a good soul trapped in the evil community, with an evil boyfriend), and she feared that he was going to attempt murder of Randy. Her boyfriend was Keith Natsch and he was evil. But somewhat more interesting what that Keith was one of the contacts on the Physics lab notepad.

The "weird/odd" accidents continued in the suburbia towns of Long Island. Randy's family friend had two kids and was married for some years. One evening, the Mets were playing baseball. Bruce enjoyed watching baseball games with his four-year old daughter. They snuggled together on a big living room recliner chair and were watching the Mets play the Braves. It was a season opener. As they comfortably watched the baseball game that evening, his wife marched toward them. He did not notice anything odd until the metal vacuum pole was hacked into the side of his temple. The kid went flying off the chair as Bruce took an additional five to ten hacks with his wife's brutal blows. That night, Bruce died of head trauma. His body was taken to the University hospital and later "disappeared". Coming home after months of training and isolation (by design, courtesy of the United States Bootcamp rule book), he expected, no – hoped to be greeted by the lady who had spent countless nights writing lyrics to love enriched country songs by George Straight, Garth Brooks. Not just lyrics, the words were accompanied with "hope" of a future and it was sealed in many perfume drenched heart-felt envelopes. Pretty cool for a young soldier in total isolation. While buddies were receiving "the dear john letter" (as they call it when the letter says:

hey "the relationship is over"), this young guy was reading love letters. That was pretty much the only form of communication for three long months. The time felt like three years, that I can assure you. Grueling, cruel and intense most of the time – tough stuff, physically and psychologically. Meeting great recruits from different parts of the United States that shared the love for "football", and the "experience" of sports, helped immensely.

Back at University

Ivanka was excited to start the spring semester – she was studious like that. What was more exciting though was to find out what was happening in the basement of the physics building. She wondered what in the hell Michael was up to with his anti-matter "experiment".Randy and Ivanka were lab partners in an early morning organic chemistry class. 7 AM to 1 PM was the class; something brutal, tough with hours (especially for a student), and curriculum was fierce. Randy missed the first week of classes. He was ordered to a command with the U.S. Navy. Ivanka wasn't completely sure what Randy was doing; as a US Navy Reservist. She knew of some "training" he was involved in. He fit the "military style", polite – a crew cut hair style and a military bearing…. But that was the extent of her familiarity with what he was doing. She also liked the many buttons on his dress uniform….

9/11 had recently occurred and most people stopped flying. She remembered one of Randy's conversations: it was just after 9/11, literally….the training orders had been in place prior to 9/11. It was important to squeeze in the active training before the fiscal year ended in October. This was a military

requirement (both financially and
within Navy regulations). Randy
boarded the plane from JFK, heading
to a destroyer squadron in Mayport
Florida. The plane was big and the
passengers consisted of four people!
No one was flying after 9/11 and
the state of fear was immense. The
people on board the plane looked at
one another with extreme paranoia.
Military personnel are trained to
travel with "ghost protocol". That
is, to travel with discretion….no
display of military coats, military
hats, etc. Not all military travelled
this way. It was common for some to
travel in full uniform; and that
was nice to see. However, depending
on the orders – most travelled low
key, in a discrete fashion.

The travel down to northeast
Florida was quick, about four and
half hours. He purchased a rent
a car with his government credit
card and headed east to the base.

Defcon 3 was promptly implemented after 9/11. Getting on base was not easy; full search of the vehicle and the people coming on base. Even with presentation of military identification.The destroyer squadron consisted on a group of battle ships with various capabilities. They were equipped with tomahawk missile capability. Very accurate missile arsenal, with sea to land target capabilities. The ships went out, heading to the waters off the coast of Iraq, in battle group patterns with "trained personnel".

Training is great, training is intense and almost "impossible" to complete. Yet, the warrior heart completes the training only to realize that there will come a time to "utilize" the training. No one really prays to utilize such military training. However, it is used with discretion, with extreme caution as "a protective force". Protection against what? There are evil groups around the world that want to literally "destroy" the United States "way of life". These evil groups are savage, with little regard for life, liberty and the pursuit of happiness. Little regard for legacy, for children, for family…..little regard for "life on Earth".

Prior to leaving the United States military ship, traveling through the rough Atlantic ocean Randy spent some time in a local bar. Sailors love a good beer and music. Some like the "strip clubs". With the attached element of beer and drinking. Randy was low key; enjoyed the beer and the sensuality (with no contact). It was probably the fact that in another part of his life he was a science guru, also a complete germaphobe! That could be a good thing…. He thought, maybe?

It was the funniest thing though, that at a young age of 18 this kid was allowed to defend and protect the interests of a great nation; The United States of America. He could not legally drink a beer? Interesting, he chatted with his military buddies on how they could maybe petition for a privilege to drink (place it on the military ID), especially prior to heading out to another circle of hell (heading into harm's way). There was never peace with war. In fact, peace rarely existed in the 200+ years of modern United States freedom. Statistically, every four to seven years there was a significant conflict. The thing is that most people did not know this. Randy's father knew this. His dad was a "survivor of the Vietnam war". His dad appreciated life and understood that "every day was a blessing" in this cruel world. In fact, Randy came from a military family, where on his mother's side, his Grandfather proudly served in the US Navy as an electrician. The "briefings" were clear to Randy and real. Most warriors were "mobilization ready" and knew very well that these statistics meant little rest. The briefings rarely made it to the civilian news networks. So, Randy would return to civilian status and not hear any word of the potential "real conflicts" that were unfolding each month, each year….

The ships discretely, with ghost protocol (circle william, battle grey, horizon invisible), traveled off the coast of Iraq. The teams conducted their ordered missions, with hover crafts, "trained personnel" and precision tomahawk mission support. Upon return to the states, Randy anxiously and happily returned to University. The peace and warmth of Ivanka's hug, kiss (French style, that he loved) and flowing shiny hair calmed his nerves. He was happy to be home. He wished he could talk more with Ivanka about the "ordered missions"; he could not.Science was the predominate major at University. However, the students were also taught to be "well rounded", to appreciate other areas of global culture. It helps put perspective on thought processes, and helps with meeting a variety of real-world challenges. Randy also studied sociology (South America and Marriage in the Family, for example). He even enjoyed playing the alto sax in the University community ensemble. Ivanka shared this love of music. Music could and has "moved world armies", music could and has created an atmosphere for "creative thinking", for "creative writing", for "creative innovation", etc. The time during the years of University study was paralleled with the birth of "alternative-grunge music". It was a new sound, it was amazing, it was innovative and the sound sparked the creative mind-set. Bands like "Weezer", "Sum 41", "Nirvana" and "Green Day" (amongst other great bands) were leading the way with this new sound. When challenged with the fiercest of competition at University, studying the most complex formulas of Einstein and the depths of biological and chemistry sciences; do what the innovative thinkers do…..listen to "Nirvana" and study! This helped fuel understanding of complex concepts, this approach helped spark creative thinking and understanding, this music was "innovative"!

Ivanka was enrolled in a music history/theory class with Randy. They were tasked with learning classical composers, their music and their styles. Tests were not easy. In fact, the tests consisted of listening to a small minute or two sample of music. Then, the music must be identified (the composer, the title of the music piece and the year of composition). It was no surprise that Ivanka was a wiz at these challenges; she truly was a brilliant soul. Randy did well too, but he had to work diligently at the exercises in order to make the grade – and that was okay…. Most students quickly realized that it is was no walk in the park. Especially, at a competitive University campus. Countless hours were spent with earphones in the University music library, listening to classical composers.

Back to the science: Randy and Ivanka were working together on molecules called "ketones" – the type of molecules that resulted in the aroma of strawberry and bananas…. Pretty cool to work with these types of solutions. I mean, who doesn't enjoy the aroma of strawberries and bananas? Maybe

Randy was thinking about the annual University strawberry fest (strawberry daiquiris, chocolate strawberries, strawberry shots, all kinds of strawberries); yeah, pretty cool. Ivanka was a rebel, working quickly with little supervision – and she spilled the ketone solutions all over her hands. The lab ended and they agreed to get together in the evening at the main lecture hall, across campus at 8 PM. The goal was set to get closer to the physics basement experiment.

Later that night, Randy was in the lecture building searching for Ivanka. He quickly realized she was in the building when he caught the aroma of strawberries and bananas! It had been 7 hours since the lab ended earlier that day and the scent from the spilled solution was still noticeable on her skin! They laughed about it, in a geeky science nerd way – but it was truly hilarious.

He loved her "light heart", with all the technical and complex thinking – Ivanka was a cute, funny soul. She loved to flirt, loved to love, and loved to giggle – it was cute, she was "peace and serenity" to Randy…. Which was something cherished and appreciated to a soul that sadly knew the horrors of war.

Heading to the physics building the evening of the botched strawberry banana experiment

It was getting late on a Monday evening when Ivanka met Randy in his dorm room. She had a key to his room and entered while Randy was sleeping. She gently crawled into bed with him and massaged his trapezoid muscles, gently. He woke to this and smiled. Her perfume was "sweet" and her hair was soft and shiny. Love was shared, and it seemed that time stopped. Love with her always entered a place and time that was "out of this world…."

Perhaps words cannot describe the love they shared; and that was certainly a good thing.

Heading out of the dorm, Ivanka and Randy were determined to find out what the hell was happening in the basement of the University Physics building. Walking across campus, they marveled at the "energy" displayed, as students walked from one building to the next. The energy supported the creative mind-set, the spirit of innovation. They opened the physics building lobby door with their electronic pass card. The building seemed empty, and that made sense since it was approaching 10 pm. Outside the basement physics lab they noticed that the lab door was propped open. Slowly, they walked toward the door. Peeping inside the lab, they did not see anyone. They entered and immediately started looking around for clues.

At the back of the lab they noticed a "booth". The booth was rectangular in shape and exhibited clear/see through walls. It was large in size and inside was a table that had a glowing reagent. The glow was bright yellow/green. The sign on the booth read: "Danger, Transport Module". They did not want to stay long since it was clear that Michael would return soon. On the lab bench they noticed two post-its. The following names were scribbled on the paper: Keith Natsch (Russia contact) and Tracey & Roe Nova (Patchogue Ambulance contact). Randy and Ivanka jotted the contact names on a piece of paper and abruptly left the physics lab. Besides the curiosity, they still were just University students. They were fatigued from long study sessions and long lectures and long laboratory sessions. In their minds (without having to verbally state words to each other), they knew what each was thinking.

Ivanka thought "let's get back to Randy's dorm, snuggle, love then fall asleep in one another's comfort". They woke the next morning. Their love never diminished with a night sleep, with a day apart, with a week or more apart. Their love was true; as true as true can be – their souls were pure, were connected from another place, another time. They shared that.... It wasn't anything that could be accurately described with words. They just knew it. When a roaring 1920s song played on the radio, a sparkle appeared in each other's eyes.... They knew that some how they had been in a night club, together sharing a drink and enjoying that music (De Ja Vous).

Early that morning they shared a shower together. The Irish spring soap was a favorite. They enjoyed the scent. Showers were not sexual (not usually), but more of a way to deepen their connection with each other. They shared that often (not every day), and enjoyed each other's company. Perhaps it was the clean refreshing water rolling over their bodies or her glistening pretty wet hair appearance that Randy always noticed, as they helped lather one another's skin. Gently with the connection of pure love; true love – no connection is more powerful on this earth.

The University campus sprang to life as the start of the spring semester unfolded. It was not all pure academics. There were clubs to join, sports to play and festivals to attend…. To name a few. Randy was involved in a student Veterans organization. Many great warriors were part of this organization. His friend, Alex was the President and a battle hardened marine from the desert storm war. Alex was happy to be back in the University community. He had recently completed training in a Midwest desert. He hated the scorpions and the training was intense, coordinated with different branches: U.S. Army, U.S. Marines and U.S. Naval Seabee construction units.

The purpose of the weekly student Veterans meeting was two-fold: search for more recruits and get ready for the annual "roth regatta race". Randy was the "secretary" of the organization, helping Alex with many different campus events. The rules of the race were simple: build a boat out of card board and duct tape; nothing else. Make sure it floats and get a skipper to race the boat from one end of a campus pond (outside Roth dorms) to the other end. Sounds simple, not so easy though. Try competing with the engineer or physics departments! The boats that were built varied in shape and size, but they were all constructed of only cardboard and duct tape. The race would take place in early spring and Ivanka would be in it too; that excited Randy. Racing together. Ivanka was in a pre-med student club that always built a pretty good construct for the race. She actually enrolled with two different teams: the pre-med team and the student athletic club.

It was mid-week, early evening. Ivanka and her Russian friends met Randy in the food court on campus for dinner. He always enjoyed having dinner with Ivanka. She spoke Russian to her friends while they ate and Randy had no idea what they were saying. Although, her brilliance could be sensed in the manner she spoke – the way she used her hands to gesture, the look in her eyes. But, mostly it was a light conversation with lots of funny jokes, laughing and flirtation; good company.After dinner, Ivanka and Randy walked over to the Physics building. They wanted to return to the basement to get more of an understanding of the "transport module". The lab was dark and empty when they arrived. The "booth" contained a few clearly marked "transport module operating manuals", nothing to technical – hand written with summary notes. After entering the small room (the booth), and reading some of the manuals, they realized there was much more to this transport module than they thought. For example, the booth was just the entry point to another area. After entering the booth, the instructions summarized how to enter the access code, to enter the next area. The access code? A post it-note, next to that instruction stated: "be CAUTIOUS; remember the chain reaction of $E=mc2$".

Ivanka was brilliant, she glanced at the access code entry and at the equation…. She recalled that the "change in energy" equals the change in mass, times the speed of light, squared. The speed of light was a constant in the equation, and that must be the access code…. What was the speed of light constant again? 186000 miles per second. That's how fast light travels and that was the entrance code, because it was the only "constant" in the equation (a value that never changed). They entered the numbers and a loud pressurized sound was immediately heard at the back of the booth. The wall opened to a corridor. They grabbed flash lights, located in the booth, and entered the dark corridor cautiously together – holding hands.

As they approached the end of the long, wide tunnel they entered another laboratory. It was spacious with a lab bench and a large gowning airlock. The airlock entry was locked with another code. They did not stay long. Their gut feeling was that there was something very sinister in this place, to secretive and the "protocol book" they found on the lab bench was entitled "transport instructions to the other side, Chernobyl". This frightened them, but what was more puzzling was the possibility that Michael had figured out a way to pragmatically apply the E=mc squared formula to transport people to another place and/or another place and time. Was that really even possible? Ivanka being the adventurous type, the curious brilliant personality type was intrigued. She wanted to stay longer, but knew that there was too much risk at this point in time. Randy said to her that he loved that about her, the adventurous personality, which was a great quality in a lady.

If you want to be adventurous, join the United States military. We need some new recruits, want to enlist with uncle Sam? She giggled, and said no, that's your thing and I know you have to catch a MAC flight out of Republic airport Friday at 10 PM. He admired her, especially for the way she cared about him. She reminded Randy that he really needed to get ready for that military trip. The orders were already cut and it was his thing. He giggled at Ivanka and smiled: you know me well and thank you for caring. You know I live the "Indiana Jones life", military operational orders and an academic in civilian life. Wouldn't it be something if one day I became an adjunct professor, similar to Harrison Ford? Wouldn't that be the perfect life of adventure, with a foundation in academia? She smiled, let's get out of here and get some rest. You up for snuggling, Indiana? They got back to the dorm and fell asleep with ultimate snuggling – bare skinned from the waist up – nothing sexual, he was a gentleman, and a Casanova-type (harmless, just enjoyed the smile of a lady). The connection between Ivanka and Randy was heavenly.

Words aren't able to describe the connection in any accurate way. The connection was always genuinely felt and grew stronger with each wonderful night they embraced together. Maybe it was her hugs, maybe it was her ambience (glowing love). But really it was more. Randy had the ability to sense where some energy came from. It was clear that the energy between Randy and Ivanka not only began during the time at the University. It was initiated in another place and time. The connection began at some point between the years 1920 and 1945. Yes, they shared this incredible feeling, it was pure happiness. The spark between Ivanka and Randy was further brightened as their shared vision was enhanced when music from the early 1900s was heard.

Ivanka brought Randy to the back of the Long Island Republic airport, where the "flights don't take off". This was a secret area, restricted only for military flights. There was a marine military jet waiting there. The jet held about 15 people, plus two pilots. Top gun movie stuff! She was excited at the sight of the "MAC, military air craft". Randy kissed Ivanka good bye and said: be back soon. A hug, kiss with her soft hair brushing his face – a memory that he would bring with him as he carried out the "mission". They would always share the memory of her soft lips together with his lips. He loved her and he knew that he would always be there for Ivanka. For many reasons: they shared something so heavenly that words can not accurately describe the connection. He understood her brilliance and he loved her brilliance. She understood Randy's past, present and loved him, cared for him and would always protect him as they moved into the future. He aspired to learn from her and cherished the way she shared her affection and sensuality through many nights they were together – it was enchanting and heavenly, always.

Randy, with his military buddies entered the MAC aircraft and sat quickly. Within minutes they were ready to take off. The two young military pilots were in training. The best of the best; how do you think they are so good? (A) they have natural talent and (B) they use it flying to every God forsaken place. How y'all doing? Welcome aboard boys; ready to get down to Virginia? They took off and were at the Little Creek Naval Base within what seemed minutes. Randy wondered what in the world type of jet engine was in this bird.

The travel was usually late at night or around midnight. This was the way to travel, typically. Even though travel was late, the units always reported on the drill deck for muster at 715AM – the next day. That's just the way it was. Randy and his unit reported to the USS Pensacola. Navy ships were enormous. Compare and contrast it to a commercial Carnival cruise liner. The carnival cruise ship is big.... Well, the Navy ships are two to three times that size! And the aircraft carriers…. even bigger than the Navy ships. It also depended on the ships function. The P-cola was an LSD-38 ship. Its capabilities coincided with marine operations (sea, air and land capabilities). The center of the ship was hollow, holding four large LCAC's (floating hover crafts).

The orders to support active fleet operations were semi training maneuvers with an active top secret element. The routine training consisted of fire fighting using mock fire and gowning in extremely heavy equipment. The darken ship protocol was implemented to mock survival in a chemical, biological and radiological attack. All ventilation systems were closed, lights were turned off to blend into the oceans horizon (reducing the risk of further attacks), and the official circle william protocol was followed during general quarters. The non-routine training was more involved. There were four teams; one team for each hover craft. The crafts were boarded, each with four men teams. The teams were ordered with four different missions. Randy's team left the ship in the first Hovercraft (LCAC Bravo). The mission was to hover the waters, off the coast of Long Island to collect air samples and water samples. A modern device was used to check samples for CBR levels. A chemical, biological and radiological attack was a big concern around the time, shortly after the 9/11 attacks.

Although, the protocol for these types of concerns had already been in place prior to 9/11 and are pretty much always in effect by brave men of women of the US military.While Randy was training and doing other stuff in the Atlantic ocean, Ivanka was at University excelling in the area of fitness. She was good! Ivanka had no problem running a 5K (3.10 mile run) and no problem running the 10K (6 mile run). Her goal was to achieve the ½ marathon. That was approximately 17 miles of intense cardio! Impressive! During time apart, they thought of each other every night and day. Randy could not call her for obvious reasons and although she didn't have all the logistical information about her loves whereabouts, her heart sensed that he was okay.

The first circle of Hell

There were many good people in the Patchogue-Medford district, this was true. What was also true though, some of the good people were "unsuspecting victims". Others were not victims because, sadly they were part of the evil – allowing it to flourish by ignoring its very existence. There was a newspaper delivery guy named Keith. A guy that just rubbed people the wrong way. For example, he was in charge of the billing for local Patchogue-Medford residents. And the community seemed to love to complain about the incorrect bills. He was over charging for newspaper delivery by a whole five extra dollars, each week! The problem with this circle of hell was that the community of evil owned homes, owned businesses, collected pensions from NY state. In fact, the circle of hell had expanded to the upper echelons of the NY state assembly, even to senator levels! Outrageous but very true. Why would one not disagree with the statement: the evil was fueled by the community, the evil was fueled by the support of the state: you see, NY state was a sanctuary state; and every criminal knew that very well. NY State was, what the psychiatrists called "enablers". Enablers for the sustainability of crimes; crimes that even included MURDER!

Roe and Tracey owned a home near the Patchogue Medford area. Roe was a "low key" Custodian in The local school district. Roe and his wife Tracey also volunteered with the local ambulance company. It was perfect! Roe had access to the children and the school administrators. Roe and his wife also had good access to the local hospitals (in and out of the emergency rooms, whenever and wherever they went). Just put on a Patchogue Medford ambulance jacket, then come and go as they pleased! Perfect resources for MURDERES!

Roe and Tracey asked Keith to enter their home one Saturday morning, to help move a very heavy exercise bike up a flight of stairs. As Keith struggled to lift the heavy bike (located at the bottom of the stairs, under the bike) Roe was on the upper part of the bike. Tracey saw Keith struggling and while she was behind him, she slyly placed a drop of a very concentrated carcinogen that had a chemical component. The chemical absorbed quickly into Keith's skin and went straight to his heart. Within minutes Keith's heart went into an "irregular beat" and his heart STOPPED. Keith died in Roe and Tracey's house that

Saturday morning. The body was brought to the University hospital, and mysteriously disappeared within days. The hospital was located across the street from the "University". The military missions were complete, for now... for these units. The return home was peaceful, Randy slept most of the way. Ivanka missed Randy, especially since almost three weeks had passed. Randy brought a copy of his military orders to most of the professors at University. Not because it was required; it was not really a requirement – you see, the University curriculum was intense and extremely technically challenging in nature. Tough for even for the best minds. The orders were presented to class professors for "consideration". An attempt to bridge the gap for why there certainly would be a "learning curve" over the next month. Thank goodness there wasn't too many "scheduling conflicts" between University studies and ordered military missions. Where possible, the missions that could be scheduled were done so during the summer months. However, this most recent mission was of urgency (an unplanned hot itemed global event).

Time moved fast, too fast. It was now real close to Valentine's day. Randy met Ivanka in her dorm late that evening. They were happy to see each other. Valentine's day was a special day. What an incredible time to show how much you love one-another, how much you truly feel for your soul-mate. The love they had for each-other was heavenly. The love was felt without spoken words (usually). Randy approached Ivanka, noticing that the dorm was dim with lit candles. The aroma was vanilla. He loved that candle scent. What was more intriguing to Randy was the scent of sweetness and vanilla that brought his lips to the place where the scent was, on her bare neck. Being closer now he noticed she was wearing cute silky "soccer shorts" with no shirt. Just a soft, silky cream and silver colored "see-though" bra that was front snap. They smirked at one another, wide eyed and full of complete adoration for love. He giggled and said: "you're not fooling me with this type of bra this time". She said "you mean you won't struggle to unsnap, fumbling for what seemed five to ten minutes looking for the snaps on the back, like last time?"…. No, he bashfully said, this was a "futuristic bra", with some sort of front ring snapping mechanism – very cute. He approached this area with care, a warrior by day and always a gentleman at night with Ivanka. In fact, surprisingly Randy was the "shy typed guy", who typically blushed in this kind of situation.

She asked if they could play wrestle, snuggle and love for Valentines day.

Well take off your clothes soldier! After Randy removed his pants and shirt, briefly standing upright with tight boxer shorts on, Ivanka burst into tears! What did they do to you, she raised her voice in a panic! She continued to say "Please, don't give me that fifty-year gag order UCMJ bullshit!" (she was good, very bright; no military training, but knew her uniform code of military justice….and what secret operations entailed…).She gently embraced him, as she cried and kissed some obvious wounds. Between your shoulder and upper chest….there is a chunk of flesh ripped out! And below your knee, oh – what is that bruise and bloodied bump. She said "come with me now to the bathroom". With such adoration of love and caring she asked Randy to sit on the bathroom sink while she gently re-cleaned, sanitized and covered the wounds. He loved her. A gentleman could see the love that a lady has when

she does something like that. That
is, taking the time to be gentle
and care, to nurture and help with
this sort of thing. What was more
impressive though, to Randy, was
how Ivanka helped him into bed and
just rested with him.

Resting together with her head
on his chest as they fell asleep
together. Yes, Randy was happy to
be back at University with his love.
He felt safe with her. She was an
incredible lady – almost too good to
be true.The price of freedom is not
free. There are brave brothers and
sisters that prepare and implement
various military missions all the
time. Most of the time people do
not know what really is happening.
However, they should know that
the price of freedom is not free.
Training accidents happened, and
those were tragic. Missions had
inherent risks. Not everyone returns
the way they were when they first

went out to defend "freedom". Some give the ultimate sacrifice and those that do are the true heroes of this great nation, The United States of America. Freedom is not free. Randy was happy to be back in an environment that was full of freedom, freedom to learn. And freedom to sleep peacefully with his true love – Ivanka.

Return to the physics basement, into the corridor and beyond

The campus was closed during "spring break". Most staff flew home to visit family during this time. Most students that were local went home or went on vacations to the Carolinas, Florida and Mexico. The on-campus labs were usually closed. However, the campus still had life. There were many students from other parts of the globe that did not fly home during this short break. They relaxed on campus and usually spent some time catching up on studies.

This was the perfect time to go back to the basement of the Physics building. Ivanka and Randy were better prepared this time around. They brought school bags with supplies, some snacks and left for the physics building around midnight, at the start of spring break. Walking across campus together was always peaceful. They enjoyed one-another's company. Holding hands, they walked slowly across campus toward the large Physics building. They noticed that there were students walking about, heading back to their dorms or just enjoying the night air. Some custodian staff were spotted in the distance. And a couple of bodies rolling a large shaped beer barrel into a dorm. They seemed to be as discreet as they possibly could be, considering the campus was supposed to be "dry".

Arriving at the side door of the large Physics building, they entered. The building was desolate, and the basement was dark – with the exception of standard dim hallway lights. The lab door was closed for "spring break". The entrance to the door was locked. Luckily, the door had an electronic entrance pad and most students (the ones that spent ample time in the laboratories) had access. As they entered the lab they were relieved to see a check list for the closing of lab operations during the spring break week. This was "verification" for their minds that no lab personnel would be visiting while they were "searching around". They entered the first airlock with the access code, as they had done during the previous visit. The code for the speed of light constant, in the E = MC squared equation worked. Traveling down the dimly lit corridor led them to the next laboratory. This is where they spent more time collecting "information/ clues" as to what exactly was going on down here. The manuals were clearly marked as "transport modules" and the equation that was highlighted in capital letters was "PV = NRT". Ivanka processed the formula quickly and brilliantly. She stated that Michael had figured out a way to take a "technical formula" and apply it to a devious, secretive plan. Reading all the manuals verified that this part of the lab was used as a transport to another place. An Island off the coast of Long Island.

An important part of the formula was the "temperature". Traveling through the module would increase human body temperature as the pressure was decreased. There were some "constants" that were placed in the formula and depending on each individuals "weight", the temperature of their body would fluctuate. Randy listened to Ivanka's summary of the transport formula, and marveled at her ability to process such "technically complex information"; in a cute way - of course. But, more importantly he trusted her. There was transport "thermal under garments" that needed to be worn during transport. The thermal material kept the human body temperature "fairly stable" during the pressure fluctuations in the transport chamber.

They followed the instructions, removing their clothes and placing undergarment thermal clothes on. The thermal clothes did not cover the entire body, just like wearing a bikini and swim trunks - except it was "high tech stuff" (they hoped....). There were additional notes about gender differences. They laughed - knowing very well that the anatomy and physiology of "a male" vs. "a female" was not much biologically different (strictly in terms of science). Michael's lab not only lacked the moral standards of the human race….but after reading through some scribbled notes, it seemed that the lab was also very "sexist"! The human body is composed of trillions of cells. The cells are arranged into "tissues", these tissues have more organized functions in the "human body". The human "tissues" are further arranged to form "organs/higher ordered systems" = these systems in the "human body" have anatomical and physiological functions that provide/sustain human life as we know it. The critical systems include: the circulatory system (the heart, blood flow, etc.), the respiratory system (the lungs, exchange of de-oxygenate blood with oxygenated blood, and its flow), The digestive system (processing of nutrients that we eat), The urinary system (maintenance of blood pH and flow of liquids we drink, etc.), The bones/connective tissues (skeleton, and within this system, blood cell maintenance, immunology, etc.), the nervous system (brain and body nerves – communication of all systems through electrical stimulus, etc.) and of course the reproductive systems (male and female parts, cycles, etc.).

So, Ivanka being the brilliant science lady she was – laughed at the sexist annotations. What a joke, to think the male and the female are so different. Biologically speaking, not too many differences when it came to anatomy and physiology! Truth be told, there were very few differences and those differences made for an incredible level of companionship for each other and for humanity as we knew it. Those differences (diversity) made the human race stronger, brighter with the potential to achieve-together the greatest of challenges. Some obvious differences were there – the male and female parts, the motherly love of a female, the protection of the female for her mate (her husband), and the protection of the male for his mate (his wife). What it really came down to was the differences in a person's "soul". There was no way to pretend to have the light of a "good soul". Eventually, the human soul will know the truth and the truth will shine from one soul to the next soul – the goodness will be evident. Sadly, the ones that do not have a good soul will also exhibit their evil nature, sooner or later. And living in the circle of hell (Long Island), there were too many soul-less shit heads walking around, enjoying the freedoms of a good "United States" culture. They entered the transport chamber, following the instructions inside the vessel. Re-entering the code 186,000 (speed of light constant) and after entering their height/weight into the central computer system – they were quickly transported. Upon arrival to the next transport station they realized that they were in another facility. After exiting the transport vessel, they observed another lab with a stack of dead bodies; each tagged with detailed information. The books located on the desk near the bodies listed each name, date of birth, residence, insurance company contact and the amount awarded to the beneficiary. The beneficiary and amount of life insurance was highlighted.

Some adventure so far! Ivanka and Randy figured out how to apply an E=mc squared formula to a real life transport vessel and immediately discovered dead bodies! It was a lot to digest, to overwhelming... They wanted to leave, but first collected some information: they found information about the facility. It was located on an island off the coast of long island (previously called "Plum Island"). The island was now deserted, with the exception of a stack of dead tagged human bodies. There was also another transport module in the facility that had instructions for transport to a nuclear hot zone in Russia (Chernobyl).

Randy suggested that they get the hell back to the University (no pun intended because although Long Island was a circle of hell, the University was one of the few places where light remained). After they returned to the University, Ivanka wanted to get off Long Island to clear her mind. She asked if they could travel to Randy's parent's place in the Adirondack Mountains for a couple of days. There they could relax, talk about what they discovered and plan/at least decide what they were going to do about all of it.The Adirondack mountains was a quick trip from Long Island. Within seven hours they were at his parent's summer place. Although, it was winter and very chilly with snow – they enjoyed each other's company. Randy started a fire in the living room fire place, the warmth relaxed them. They shared a bottle of wine. And after that….a few more bottles of wine. The occasional drink (maybe a bit more than occasional) relaxed their electrically stimulated minds. Randy was a silly drunk, as was Ivanka – not that they were planning to get completely "wasted on boos"….they laughed and called it a "semi-drunk state….". Both were well aware of their surroundings, the warmth of the fire place and the softness of each other's kisses. She was always sensual, full of a remarkable amount of energy – that fascinated Randy.

He was similar with sensuality and energy, during love. It was the way they took care of each other that was also remarkable. The love was more than just a superficial motion of events. It was everything. Her gentle kisses on his ear, her tongue that searched for something in that area (an ear drum?). The passion was amazing.Afterwards, they rested together under the sheets - bare skinned. Her head resting on his chest, talking about life. You know Ivanka, you could have just given me a "hickey" to mark your territory! She giggled and said that she was "passionate", she needed to do more to mark her territory. He said "oh". Ivanka replied: well, maybe I just enjoy using my finger nails…. The thing is that prior to leaving on military "missions", we are given a thorough exam and we stand "bare assed", at attention. Last time, the group had their share of laughter when they observed the deep scratch marks in my back skin, from you! She giggled and replied: my territory soldier! They laughed and fell asleep together, in total comfort – true love, a piece of heaven on Earth.

The next day they spoke about the transport module and what they needed to do. Some things were just outside of the routine jurisdiction of "societal law". They decided to go back through the portals to see if the portal actually went to "Russia". The labs had radiation safety devices and suits, and they brought all that with them when they transported.The transport was so easy, incredible for such an advancement in technology. Imagine what this could be used for! In the area of "Chernobyl" there was an "evil presence". It certainly was guarded by some sort of evil entity. As they exited the last portal, they read the radiation gauges and did not see any increases in levels.

Outside of the lab there was a large iron gate that lead into the most-evil environment they had ever placed their eyes on. It was truly a scene from "Dante's Inferno".

Prior to entering the evil gate, Randy and Ivanka noticed various bright lights surrounding the dark land. The brightness was caused by the presence of angelic figures: a protective force. These "angels" guarded the entrance. Randy recognized two of the figures: a family member and a warrior friend. Both who had crossed over to Heaven – years ago. They approached Randy and Ivanka. The angels advised them to take care, take extreme caution, if they chose to enter the evil gates.

The angelic family explained of the presence of these bright lights. They shed light on the circle of hell that existed on Long Island, the depth of the murderous events, the fact that it had been an evil presence for the past fifty years. The bodies that were transported into the gates were not transported "in whole". The most important area of self was removed by the angels. The souls of each murdered victim was being saved by these angels. The angels could not enter the gate, but they could save the souls of each victim, and bring them to heaven. Catholic religion taught that "re-incarnation" did not exist. Randy and Ivanka were "scientific" and "religious", which helped them keep an open mind. Crossing over is a mystery, a mystery of faith. Not many know exactly what happens. Some have had near death experiences, with some visions. Randy and his buddies entered a military war/conflict on Earth in the year 2001. No one asks for war, and when it happens – the conversation must be had with "your maker". That conversation is one of peace, to ask for protection while preparing to enter "harms way", to ask for "forgiveness of Earthly sins", and to humbly thank the "maker" for all Earthly blessings over the years. The conversation "switches" the warrior. Each brother and sister enter the conversation as one type of person, then exits the conversation as "another type of person". The change is a good change because it provides a deeper understanding of life, with the "acceptance" of what may happen as the warrior enters "harm's way".

The angels spoke of a "choice" that were given to some souls. The souls that endured great suffering and great harm on Earth were given the "choice" to travel back to Earth as a "new born baby". Or, the "choice" could be to stay near the gates of heaven as a "protective angel". There was no pressure to choose and time was not the same as it was on Earth. The choice could be made by these souls, or they could head into the gates of Heaven. What happened there was still a mystery of faith.Ivanka and Randy thanked the angels, as they wiped tears of joy and emotion from their eyes. The wisdom from these angels was a bit overwhelming. The emotions that were elicited were great and awesome in nature. Ivanka and Randy hugged each other and talked about the souls that were being saved. They discussed what they needed to do, and that was to enter this gate of hell (this one gate, there were most likely many other gates of hell on Earth). The angels said "stay safe", we will help as best we can.

After entering the gate of hell, Ivanka and Randy felt sick and scared. They looked at each other and paused for a moment. Ivanka grabbed the golden cross from her necklace and smiled. They moved forward to the base of the large, dark mountain and started climbing upward....

The Darkness of Pure Evil

This is the part of the adventure that is full of challenges, uncertainty and potential danger, are you ready "adventurous lady"? Ivanka responds: "I've been ready my whole life". We move forward, then stop. Randy states: "you trust me? please, let's stop and quickly brief one another on what we are about to get ourselves into...." This is dangerous, we are entering an area of "pure evil", and we will be submerged in it with the risk of not returning. You see, the evil is not one person, like they say. At least, not on Earth. The evil is a state of atmosphere, an entity that is not intelligent – in the sense that a "person can speak about it". The evil is a fog of pure evil elements that gets absorbed into the human spirit. And if the human soul is not strong enough to repel it, well then – the person carries out evil without even having a sense that he/she is doing the evil tasks. How do I know this? I don't know, I just do – it's a gift, or a curse (depending on how you look at it). A curse because it certainly can be overwhelming on the heart, at times.

The "briefing continues…". Trust me that we need to absolutely remember (always remember, no matter how evil things get) that (A) we proceed together, hand in hand, heart in heart, together as we face whatever is ahead of us. Okay? She replies – yes, of course, that's a constant, like in a physics equation! (giggling). Good, but stop with the giggles, this is not funny, you see – we move forward and we need to stop this evil entity – this is above Earthly law. We are tasked with it and there is a chance the evil will consume us, and we will not return. You understand? Therefore, stay brilliant – you are, I know that, but trust in the next part of the briefing: no jokes = (B) we proceed cautiously with the cross of gold around your neck and what it represents (that is = all the good of our God, his angels and the mother Mary). This is key to our success, without your cross, we are lost.

And (C) we rely on our training, the might of the warrior spirit and your brilliance. There may be times where we need to "take action", but typically – we need to proceed cautiously, with the remembrance of strategy (A, B, C !) and smartly with the reliance of intense historical training; the might of the military spirit (trust me). They look at one another with goodness, and sense of panic. You look scared? So do you? Good, we know what we are getting ourselves into, and that is half the battle. Let's finish the other half of the battle; destroy the evil entity here – and then return home, to the University….The mountain consisted of five very distinct levels, separated by obvious shades of mist. Furthermore, there were etched signs seen (in stone) with the following descriptions: I. Society, II. Farm Country, III. The Football Field, IV. Iraq, V. Source. Entrance into the first level was not like entering a door to a house. It just happened as they moved through the mist. The level eventually appeared to them and they were not just spectators to the surroundings. No, they were actually in this foreign land. This was mysterious and a bit overwhelming, since they did not know where they had traveled to and how they would get back.

Remember, the briefing: your cross, our strengths together with might of intense training! Smile! They did, kind of....

Level One of the Dark Mountain within the Gate of Hell

They were at a dinner table, in a nice Long Island restaurant. The people were familiar to Randy and they spoke to him as well. It was a group of pharmaceutical techs that had gotten together for a holiday dinner. As the conversations continued, they were able to see past the walls where the food was being prepared. And hear the cook babbling about one dish that was going to an individual.... The babbling was psychotic, not rationale – an evil wind had prevailed, it was sort of a "devil's dinner" because one individual had been targeted. The coordinator was the head of the techs that had access to stock pots of biological toxins from nasty microorganisms. The stocks were large populations of E. coli that had a toxin that could bypass the human blood brain barrier, causing shock – and eventual death within hours of ingestion.The food was brought to the table and they began eating. The targeted individuals name was "Joe" and he ate all his tainted food. Within an hour he was feeling ill and excused himself. Randy and Ivanka followed him to his car, where he complained of his temperature (rapid temperature fluctuations, cold, hot, headaches, etc…) They frantically tried to help him…. he died within the hour. The mist swept in and another evil vision appeared: the body of Joe being transported to the University, the portal and out to Chenobyl, Russia. The last vision of this scene was a suburban house wife holding a check for 1 million dollars and not crying, but smiling. The evil mist flowed in this level of the mountain, bringing Ivanka and Randy to a church. In the church groups of people were meeting in a "devil's conference". It was clear that the elements of society on Long Island were using the sanctity of marriage, gender and religion to propel their evil plans. It was sad to Ivanka and Randy. To see such a network of evil, summarized in one "devil's conference". The evil network was connected and thrived in good areas of suburbia.

Level Two: Farm Country

The farmland of Long Island was nice to see. The mist seemed to have washed away the evil atmosphere of level one, propelling them up to the second level of the mountain. The land was open, with green cabbage farms and corn stalks as far as the eye could see. Judging from the mild to cool breeze and bright blue sky, it was early autumn. Similar to the previous level, this was no illusion. No, Ivanka and Randy were there, in some suburban town. In the distance they could see a sign: "barnsly crescent, Mt. Sinai NY". The road was a suburban road, a small town next to farms. A school bus approached from the distance, where children exited. The kids ran to their houses anxiously, leaving thoughts of school behind. A young boy, about the age of eight ran to them: "wanna climb that tree?", he did not wait for them to answer, he was eager to climb a large birch tree. The tree was located directly in front of his house. And was almost sixty to eighty feet tall!

He started climbing the tree. As they watched him climb, they could see other visions that the mist brought their way: sort of an explanation of what the boy was thinking. He loved to climb the tallest of trees.

It was a calling from deep within his good soul. No words, just inner direction from a source of goodness. A gift from the good lord. As he got higher in the tree, he could feel the effects of the breeze sway the tree. That brought his attention to grab closer to the trunk and climb more cautiously. At the top of the tree the boy reflected and observed all the beauty the eyes could see. What a view!

The nice view and the tree did not last long, the wind of evil prevailed in this second level. Ivanka and Randy watched in horror and could feel the shift in atmosphere. A shift from pleasantry to a sickness of evil. The boy started descending down the tree. About halfway down, an evil wind gusted and threw off his sense of coordination and balance. The boy fell, hitting tree branches along the way. Eventually, he was flat on his back on the ground below. Miracles do happen though, and the boy was to young to realize. He had been blessed with some heavenly protection…..he survived, with no more than some scrapes and bruises. He limped into his modest, one-story house….

Shortly after viewing this level of evil, Ivanka and Randy found themselves on a ledge – at the side of the mountain, just above level 2, but below level 3. They talked: what are we experiencing? The levels seemed to be some organization of evil that has transpired over time. The evil detected a soul that was"good", with "heavenly ability". And with these abilities, the evil set out to destroy it, but could not. Some died and the evil infrastructure and network was there. Yet, somehow this one soul prevailed. Randy turned to Ivanka, approaching her pretty face slowly. She said "what?". Ivanka, that soul depicted in these levels….that soul, that boy, ….. he is me! They continued upward to level 3: The Football Field.

Mountain Level 3: The Football Field

The experience of playing a sport is one that should be sought by most kids, most adults. Even if it is just an intramural soft ball league. The joy of it, the discipline learned, the team work, the training, …. All of it, all of it you take with you in this life. The mist brought them to a rainy, dreary afternoon. They were on the side of a football field that looked more like a farm land mud show, with farm animals. There were two football teams. One with red and black jerseys and the other with green and white jerseys. The team with the green and white jerseys were very big! Big boys with lots of blubber, lots of height. As

Randy watched the game, the evil wind showed visions of the school bus ride to the field. The team was approaching the "enemy" and in the distance they could see ropes with red/black jerseys hanging from it! The coach had the team leave their seats and congregated in the center isle with their football helmets on. The concern was that rock or other weapons would be propelled at the bus!

Randy turned to Ivanka again and stated: this is me, I recall this. Where are you? Heading into the field right now, on the line. He was not a big dude, but strong as hell. And that was a secret weapon, a good weapon to have. Speed, strength and the will to fight. The opposing guy was about six foot three inches tall, and three hundred pounds of blubber. Randy recalled being about 180 pounds, but near to pure muscle, with the ability to push up three hundred + pounds on the bench press. And squat four hundred plus pounds. Nevertheless, these opponents were evil. They did not play fair. They were out for blood. The play was to jab this fat bastard in the shoulders with extreme force – a goal of the line man was always to keep these big boys from getting to the quarter back. The problem was that this monster came into him with such force and intentionally smashed his metal spiked cleat into the top of his opponent's foot! Breaking bone/toe. Randy observed his former self limping to the side, where the coach yelled – you afraid of this team? Let's get it done, he is to big; your strong, but he's playing dirty....chop block him. The game continued and it seemed to Ivanka and Randy that this was a level of hell, where an opposing team could target any team mate, then hide behind the fact that it just was a rough sport. The winds of evil shifted and they were brought outside of level 4. Waiting and anticipating something more-evil, Randy and Ivanka held each other. Ivanka whispered, I always thought your foot looked funny to me! Giggling…. Any chance I can get a massage when we get back to University, for my sore foot? Giggling…

Mountain Level 4: Iraq

The equipment used in military operations is amazing. Some of it seems to defy traditional physics. Many hours were spent marveling at the military aircraft take offs, at different bases, in different parts of the world. And on different ships and air craft carriers in various oceans. The sheer ability of these aircraft to be guided with military warriors required a unique talent, intense training, experienced technique, and an immense understanding of various formulas (scientific formulas; mathematical formulas; physical formulas; environmental formulas; etc.).The chinook helicopters were massive in size and had incredible war-time capabilities. These choppers were utilized in many different conflicts and in many global operations. As the mist blew their way, Ivanka and Randy found themselves aboard a Chinook chopper flying over a desert in Iraq. They were officially in the fourth mountain level. And this level, being closer to the top, seemed very dangerous. The team on board was preparing to jump out of the chopper. There was a count down and they would jump in T minus twenty seconds. Remember Ivanka: stick together. Deep breath, jump and pull that bright red tab in "30 seconds (mississipppppp….) – got it! Just do it and don't look back. When you land, bend your knees and stay where you land. I will find you.

Two other things: (1) take this knife (slice anything that attacks you) and (2) fire this pistol straight up in the air (it is night and I will coordinate my compass and head toward you after you fire this flare straight up into the air) – got it! Fair winds and God speed lover! They jumped and into the cold night air they went, tumbling quickly downward into an abyss…. After landing in the desert sand Ivanka fired the flare straight up and waited, holding onto the knife – searching for any movement in the night sky. Randy landed and immediately observed the flare, it was some distance from where he was. His training would come to be helpful in this area of hell. His estimates brought him about four hours from her. He was trained to "cycle" (intense cardio training) for one hour, two hours, four hours, eight hours and even up to twelve hours (with some struggle). The four hour "cycle" would be tough, since it was desert sand. He removed his boots and started the run barefoot toward her.

Warming up at the start of the run was the critical part. During training this was an essential element for success. Meaning, the environment needed to be surveyed as the run commenced. Was the air thin? Was it tough to breath? Was it super cold? How was the terrain? Be one with the environment and assimilate into the environment, aligning all internal human biological systems with the outside world….running in sync with the environment, breathing accordingly, warming air (if necessary) by breathing into the shirts sleeve, then placing nose in warmed sleeve, etc. The run was not easy, this was a land that was full of pure evil, and Randy felt that. Another area of training was to calm nerves, think of a soothing song: perhaps classic rock or a good Bon Jovi tune: "bed of roses" or "always" helped slow heart rate and enter into a state of biological homeostasis (balance between all internal biological systems and the outside, harsh environment). Two hours into the cycle (the run), all seemed "on track", and Randy would be arriving to meet Ivanka soon....

As he ran in the cool desert sand, he also took some subconscious time to think about the history of this land. This part of the world had an incredible history, with unfortunate circumstance: plaque by hundreds upon hundreds of war years between religious groups. Suppression of women was also a terrible plaque on the land. To make matters worse, the savage nature of extremists in this region was at such a heightened level that it seemed to border on the line of irrationality. Savages in this land had little to no regard for human life. Blood shed was common and murders were carried out routinely.Randy had reached Ivanka by early daylight, and just in time as they were greeted by a band of savage extremists. Soldiers Randy knew were there, a unit of special operations were captured by these savages. Two were cuffed, being lowered into pine boxed coffins. The coffins were covered and nailed closed. The team was trained on this tactic of savage technique. It was a way to obtain counter intelligence. Scare the hell out of the enemy, scare them into confessing all top-secret information….

As this was happening, savages were approaching Randy and Ivanka. Calmly Randy spoke: "give me the knife darling". She replied: "What ?" slowly he repeated and said discretely, hand me the knife. She did so and as the savages approached…. they were greeted with lethal, accurate and precise slices. The cloud of evil wind immediately blew; Randy and Ivanka were no longer near these savages; they were brought to another part of Iraq (a heavy wooded forest). Her clothes were not "military style" and her hair was a pretty golden blonde with subtle waves. Not what you would expect to find in the jungles of Iraq. But, they were there and most importantly…they were still together. They started climbing on a gradual wooded incline in deep forest. Shortly, they were surrounded by a U.S. special forces team. A team that consisted of eight highly trained men, lead by their "white rabbit" (team lead). What the hell are you doing here and who is she? Randy attempted to explain, paused and then re-attempted with a different approach. The mission is covert, between the two of us. This is Ivanka – a brilliant support to the mission. We are attached to a US destroyer squadron ship, off the coast of the continent; a guided-missile vessel with tomahawk capabilities. The eight-member team spread quickly as they heard gun fire in the distance. Randy and Ivanka went with the communications guy. They were communicating with one another via an ear piece. The communications guy was "spartan". The distance to the enemy was off a ways….but they were rapidly approaching the U.S. team.

Communications outside of the forest was disrupted with the mountain terrain. This was a problem since prior mission intelligence was incorrect. The best of the best special teams have the capability to take out targets. Very large targets. However, what the intel neglected to verify was the presence of technologically advanced weapons. Spartan to White Rabbit – the two U.S. Chinooks are in route to the hot zone in T-twenty minutes. Roger that white Rabbit, over. Randy frantically raised concern to Spartan: "these chinooks will be taken out by the enemy weapons". How do you know that? I just do. Advise White Rabbit. Each chinook had at least ten to twelve military soldiers on board. The team could not communicate with the approaching U.S. Chinooks due to the mountainous forest. Communication signals were disrupted. Randy asked permission for Ivanka to take charge of communications; with the team lead "target code". This was a word or sum of various words that verified the use of deadly force: which included the most technologically advanced weapons known to this Earth. The codes always changed and were only given just prior to the advancement of each particular mission.

Absolutely not! White Rabbit, there is no time for explanation here.

We take action now or the chinooks go down and we most likely won't make it home; over. White Rabbit replied: "we do not allow unknowns in any mission and certainly no woman!" Randy replied: "this woman is brilliant, smarter than me and all of your team put together", trust me, over. White rabbit paused, briefly, then replied "White Wolf, Smoke um". Roger white Rabbit, take cover – get ready for some real shock and aw shit….Ivanka was truly a brilliant soul. Maybe it was the Russian thing, maybe it was the female thing? Who knows, but it was a fact, and Randy always would admire that about her. Ivanka ran her fingers through her long gorgeous blonde hair, removing a few pins. She asked for the communications device and went to work on the inner parts…. Within a few minutes the radio was zoning into another frequency – she raised one of the U.S. Navy war ships, located in the ocean – surrounding the war zone. Outstanding Ivanka! Let me jump in now.

Randy communicated the "White Wolf, Smoke um code" and followed with the estimated distant coordinates. Verified and implemented. Within five minutes two tomahawk missiles were accurately fired from the ships deck plates. The missiles were traveling fast toward the enemy. The enemy was approximately 2000+ savage soldiers, with tactical weapons. Randy turned to Ivanka, we always pray and hope that "training" provides us with a good estimate of "coordinates". Always prepare for the worst and hope for the best. The sound is going to be loud, with extreme force. There is a chance we are too close to the blasts. They climbed behind a large boulder, holding each other. She gazed into his eyes, kissed his forehead. Then gently kissed his nose, followed by soft kisses as their lips embraced. I love you. I love you. She snuggled deep within his chest, placed her head into one of his arm pits. The large missiles cruised over them, loudly and exploded accurately/ precisely in the distance. They were safe. The special eight member US team was safe. The two chinooks were safe.

Mountain Level 5

The evil mist instantly blew at them and they were at the top level, the mountain level 5. The area seemed peaceful and as they squinted their eyes in the darkness – what appeared….surprised them. It was a "baby's bedroom", painted in light purple, and decorated with pretty white butterflies. Care had been taken to prepare this room, and it was truly something of comfort and peace. In the room was a crib, with a six to eight-month old baby girl in it. Through the wooden crib bars, there were spaces. The baby was standing in the crib, trying to get out. A man in pajamas said: "its two in the morning, go to sleep baby", and the baby smiled at him. In her eyes the man (and Ivanka and Randy) all saw brilliance, love and affection for this man. The baby was cute and she quickly listened to this man, sitting back down in the crib. However, this smart baby knew that she was not going to sleep. No, not yet. As she lay in the crib, she placed her arm through the bar spacing….a gesture to the man. He smiles, lays down on the rugged floor next to the crib and raises his arm. He gently takes the babies hand and they fall asleep for a short time; holding hands together. Not much time passed, the baby was hungry. The man stood up and picked the baby up from the crib. He gently hugged her and brought her in close to his chest as they walked down a flight of stairs leading into the kitchen. Ivanka and Randy followed. In the kitchen, this man took care to sterilize a baby bottle with a small sterilization system. The empty bottle was hot, steaming and he added bottled water to it. After that a scoop of "similac powder" was transferred. He took care to mix the bottle properly and warm it in the microwave. He did not give the bottle to the baby, yet. It was important to ensure that the contents of the bottle were not "too hot". After the preparation, mixing and heating….he squeezed drops of baby bottle formula, from the nipple onto the back of his hand. He was ensuring that the contents were warm, but not too hot.

They were in a modest home, with a small kitchen. The appliances and the tiled floor looked charming though. The clock on the wall was reading "3 AM". They walked into the living room and sat on a comfy tan colored recliner, peacefully as this baby girl sucked her bottle of simalac nutrients. The man looked peaceful, happy, content...but also fatigued. This baby loved to stay awake through most of the night and some babies are like that. Others sleep right through the night. Yes, it was not easy....but the calmness and peace in this man's eyes showed a level of contentment, of happiness.

The wind of evil blew through this modest home and the environment instantly changed from one of calmness to dark, uneasiness. A woman with rage in her eyes appeared, and ran down the stairs screaming in utter horror. She was babbling about something irrational. Randy and Ivanka could not understand what she was angry about. The baby woke up to this violence. It got worse. As they watched, the women stormed past them from the living room into the kitchen, knocking over the sterilization system, and empty bottles – continuing to scream. The man and the baby were now standing in the living room, not far from the kitchen. Within seconds, a large hard glass candle (the long church type candles that are purchased every day from dollar stores) was picked up by the woman and propelled violently in the direction of this man and baby. He turned quickly to avoid being struck by this large object and took care to cover the baby in his arm; deep in his chest.

The large glass church candle was thrown with such force that as is flew past this man and baby, connecting with the wall behind them – it shattered into a hundred tiny glass pieces. The baby started crying and the man attempted to rationalize with this woman. There was no rationalizing – no, this was pure evil and utter sadness.

The evil wind shifted and Ivanka and Randy were moved into another area of the fifth level. A dark cave with fire to light the area. In the distance were two snake-like figures – "medusa" and perhaps her cousin? They were guarding the source of this evil mountain, the "evil black shadowed entity", located at the top of, what looked to be a church altar.

Just then two bright angels appeared and were recognized by Randy. They had been present at the entrance to the gate of this hell. The first angel was a family member. The second was a friend, a warrior who lost hist life while protecting the freedoms we all hold so dear to our hearts (US led war). The angels spoke softly to Ivanka and Randy. They stated: "your efforts have brought this evil mountain into a weakened state, and although it is forbidden for us to enter such darkness, we did it to protect the both of you". The angels each gave a large wooden rosary; one for Ivanka and one for Randy. These will be a useful tool to destroy what remains of this evil mountain. Place the rosary around the neck of each Medusa and they will be banished into the depths of hell. The one angel, a lady who had passed over to soon in this life (at the young age of fifty-one) presented additional information. She stated: "you two have been courageous, with the strength of a legion", your strengths were clear to us from the start.

Your love for each other and the way you stayed together helped us get to this level of the mountain. We thank you. Divine journeys are full of faith and you two have an incredible level of faith.There is so much more to this horror that we would like to share with you. First of all, although Angels guarded the entrance to this hellish mountain, and the souls of victims were being saved….not all souls were saved. Some of the victim's souls could not be saved. and these souls, sadly, entered intothis mountainous Hell. Once the evil here is destroyed, we have faith that the lost souls of these victims will be saved with the goodness of our Angelic light. Secondly, the mystery of faith remains just that: the mystery after the soul crosses over. However, your diligent courage has earned you a glimpse into this mystery of faith. The good souls are essentially given a choice just before entering the gates of heaven. We are all energy that is not created or destroyed, and the energy is never wasted, it is transferred from one generation to the next. The soul harnesses this energy and sometimes, "the soulmate" of an individual recognizes the other soul-mates "energy". That recognition is of a place/time somewhere else. During a time when they were together: perhaps during a time when they were sharing a drink or when they were in a loving and passionate relationship.

The energy is divine and some may choose to transfer back to an "earthly existence". Others may choose to remain as a "protective angel", to guard over friends and family. While, some choose to enter into the gates of heaven. And that is where we end this vision. Because the mystery of faith must remain "a mystery of faith". The Angels left, peacefully. Randy and Ivanka hugged. It was time to put an end to this evil circle. They moved forward into the dark/dim cave, carefully. Ivanka said: "I guess there is some truth to Greek mythology after all". And that was true, as they observed the shadowed medusa figures in the cave's distance. In darkness they recalled that they should not look directly into the eyes of the medusa figures. This would result in a victim being turned to stone, instantly. A "large shield" appeared in front of Ivanka. In the inner side of the shield was a vision of her cross being forced into the evil entity, at the top of the cave's altar. She grabbed the cross from around her neck. Randy whispered: give me your wooden rosary. He would take care of both medusas, while Ivanka battled the final dark entity.

Sometimes, evil wins. Sometimes, a heart and soul can only absorb so much darkness before it reaches a saturation point. Randy and Ivanka separated.

The first medusa was destroyed with the light of the first rosary. As this happened, it was the second medusa that aggressively attacked from Randy's blind side. The second rosary made its way to the neck of this medusa.... But, with all the hate and anguish surrounding this dark matter, the evil medusa was propelled violently to the depths of darkness...along with Randy's saturated soul. For one split second, Ivanka felt her heart skip a beat... stop for what seemed longer than it really was....then, her heart started beating again. Even though they were now not together in this large dark cave, Ivanka knew something had gone gravely wrong. As Ivanka approached the evil entity on top of the altar, the cross glowed brightly – providing the guiding force to the ultimate destruction of this evil. The dark mountain was washed away instantly, as natural wind swiftly blows debris on a cool spring morning. Ivanka was tired and "blacked out from extreme fatigue". The Angel's promptly transported the exhausted Ivanka to her dorm bed. They left with her the charred military dog tags of her lover. The tags had Randy's name, social security number and blood type etched in the metal on the top surface.

Also, on these tag surfaces were fresh tears. Inside the tear droplets Ivanka observed herself sitting outside Randy's bedroom door. The bedroom was in a house that he had spent most of his childhood in. She was sitting right outside his bedroom door, wearing a pink championship sweatshirt. The sweatshirt had the fresh aroma of a recent wash with extra snuggle soft fragrance (Randy always loved that scent on her, along with her sweet perfume and soft/silky golden hair). Ivanka sat there on the rugged floor, crying…. asking for Randy's return to her. She was pleading for his return. Pleading to not leave her alone in this dark part of the world (Long

Island)....there was no answer. She would never see her lover again. At least not in this story. A reunion of the hearts for these "soul-mates" may occur in another place, in another time....

The End (continued in chapter 2)

Chapter 2

The Long Island Horror

Richard Alexander Boehler, Jr.

Ivanka woke and immediately made her way to the bathroom. She showered with the irish spring soap that Randy loved. She showered alone. Afterwards, she took a meticulous care to remove all charred residue from her lover's dog tags. First, she needed to remove the rubber "silencer" on each tag. The silencer was treated with a chemical that enabled it to withstand the harshest of conditions. However, the true purpose of these silencers was to do just that, ensure silence. Silence the clanking of the two dog metal tags, during active military operations. Operations that sometimes required an approach that needed to be extremely silent. For example, recon missions or intelligence gathering missions. She thought long about what her next move was going to be. Continue the semester studies, continue the University classes….she could do that sort of thing, and try to forget. Although, there would always be a part of her that would be broken in this life. The two dog tags were designed for battle. One tag to be placed inside the mouth of a fallen warrior, followed with a violent kick to the jaw - leaving teeth imprints in the metal tag. One tag was then brought back to the base for identification purposes and funeral preparation (honors with a salute and presentation to next of kin). The other tag was placed on the toe of the fallen military brother or sister. Transporting to a mountain of evil, of course had not been a typical mission. Ivanka knew she needed to "take action". She was thinking...

Ivanka and Randy shared so much. She knew him well and although she did not know all the details of his training, his "missions"; she knew this: he was a fighter. She knew he would not give up. Randy would continue on until the end of time. And time was not over. One element of evil may have been destroyed, but time went on and good continued to exist. Evil continued to sadly exist to. She felt deep in her heart and in her connected soul that he was still fighting…..true love finds a way to "take action". True love does not sit back idling while one heart is lost in a jungle. True love finds a way to connect, to be together. Ivanka was going back. She would find a way to locate Randy. She did not know how she would accomplish this seemingly impossible challenge. It would start with a prayer, followed with the transport module, in the basement of the University physics building… Ivanka did not sleep as well, as she usually slept when Randy was with her. She felt alone, a part of her was missing and that created an immense amount of sadness. Ivanka was not only brilliant with academics at the University, she was also incredibly resourceful. She was a survivor. She knew that where she was headed was not a good place. It would be back to a place of pure evil. And if she was lucky, she would find Randy. Not just find him, but rescue him – bring him home. She started packing her school bag with water bottles and protein bars. She wore his dog tags around her elegant neck and then left the University. Her first stop was at the church where Randy spent his childhood. She needed to meet with "Dr. Ed", a Catholic priest with many years of experience in the church. He was also very educated in the area of theology! This would add to her resources, as she prepared to eventually transport back to the mountain of evil (or what remained of the mountain).

Ivanka arrived at the church in Medford, Long Island. It was a modest church, actually very modest in its land, parish center, chapel and main church. Ivanka had visited many "cathedral style" churches in her childhood. The University had a small chapel where some religious services were performed, but she only attended during holidays. It's not that she didn't believe in "God". She did believe. And Randy had a similar philosophy. They prayed together, they believed in "God". The University church services were every Saturday evening and every Sunday morning. They attended some of the weekend services (but not many), believing that the sacraments they had completed in the Catholic religion were important. The sacraments of baptism, communion, and reconciliation were all representative of the holy traditions in the Catholic church. Each sacrament had been completed by Ivanka and Randy. She was thankful that this priest from Randy's childhood welcomed her, with such short notice.

Ivanka arrived in the Chapel, greeted by a very friendly Irish Priest – Father Ed. He invited her into his office and spoke at great length about Randy. It was interesting to her, hearing about the many years of service that Randy participated in. He was an "altar server", meaning that he wore a nice bright white robe, nice shoes and helped the priests during church services. During Randy's time on the altar he was called an "altar boy", since there were no "altar girls". The Catholic religion was slow to offer that opportunity to women during those years of service. Things changed though, and altar boys and altar girls eventually served together at Catholic church services. Some faithful parish people asked about priests that could marry a woman in the Catholic church. The priests were gentlemen married to the faith of the church, not a woman. However, a "deacon" could perform Catholic church services (similar to the priest; with some limitations) and still have a family at home.

That is a family with kids and a wife, while serving on the Catholic altar. Ivanka was fascinated to hear father Ed lecture about the Catholic religion. After all, he was a doctor (PhD) in religious studies, and he often enjoyed talking about the subject matter.Ivanka was not going to delve into the details of her journey through space and time. Most people would not believe it and as far as the evil entity; well – there are just some things that are above the law. This was one of those things. She asked for guidance in battling "evil". She did not speak in detail, but was reaching out for "protection against the evil she was about to face". Father Ed offered her two Catholic tools. The first was blessed holy water. The water was in a clear glass container. The second tool was a blessed prayer bible. The book had summary prayers that would help protect her from evil. Ivanka thanked the priest for his time, his wisdom and the two Catholic church tools. He smiled, paused, then placed his hand on her shoulder. Looking kindly into her eyes, Father Ed softly stated: "God's speed on the journey to the dark side my child – I will pray for you and Randy". He knew of this evil, she was sure of it. She could see it in his eyes. The fear in his eyes and the understanding of how to battle such evil. Ivanka smiled back at him, then left for the University physics building.

At the University it was late and she arrived with her backpack full of supplies. Including the church tools. She double checked her resources, zipped the bag closed then entered the transport module. At the gate of the evil mountain (what remained of it) she met the lady Angel. Ivanka believed that this lady Angel was watching over her and was expecting her. The Angel spoke to Ivanka and advised her that she was heading into a very evil unknown. The place where Randy went was uncharted territory. The Angel went on to say that even if she wanted to follow her, she could not. The depth of the evil mountain is one thing. But, underneath the mountain was transportation into the circles of "Hell".Ivanka noticed a tear from the Angels eye. The Angel began to talk about Randy and her relationship to him. You see, I knew Randy on Earth prior to his entrance into the Armed Forces. He was a bit of a "wild child", and she giggled. The force was unique with him though, and he was aware of it. He often called it a "gift", and sometimes "a curse". At times, it could be overwhelming – having certain heavenly gifts (he never went into too much detail as to what the actual gifts were). He knew from the early age of about seven that he was given some interesting insights. The angel recalled dancing with him at a graduation party, Randy leaving the state and then shortly after that she entered the heavenly land as an Angel. She had sadly passed at the young age of 51. Before you go to search for Randy, please accept this necklace. The necklace held a crystal jewel that contained the light of the heavens. In this dark land, the light glowed a luminescent blue. It was spectacular. The angel offered this tool as a protective force, against the depth of hell. Ivanka thanked her, then proceeded into the mountain.

The winds of evil were less-existent. However, she still sensed a strong element of evil. As she walked away from the angel the environment changed. The sky disappeared and the lands became dark. Ivanka trembled in fear. She remembered the briefing her and Randy had before entering this evil land. This memory helped relieve some of her fear. As she stood near the area that propelled Randy to the depths of hell she started reciting a few prayers. She asked for entrance into the circles of hell. Loud noises were heard and a clear evil voice distinctively stated "go away". Ivanka continued to pray and talk to this evil voice. She repeated over and over, take me into the depths. She continued to hear "go away", Ivanka knelt down in utter defeat crying, then saying "take me to my soul mate, I love him, I need him!" – the evil entity propelled her down into the depths of hell. Perhaps, the entrance was from the help of Randy's family angel. But Ivanka thought it may have been more likely that the evil entity wanted to trap two souls in this dark place, Randy's soul and now her soul.

As she approached a large lava pit of fire, Ivanka could see a shadow in the distance. She knew that it must be Randy. Crossing over to the heavens is one thing, but plunging into the depths of an unknown circle of hell… well, she thought – there is so much uncertainty, too much evil, and little guidance at this point. Then she remembered. She did have guidance. The angel gave her a very special necklace with heavenly light bottled in crystal. She wore this around her neck and it provided her with heavenly protection, guidance and a heightened sense of her surroundings. And in her distant surrounding she knew that Randy was there. He appeared fatigued with no shirt, sweating, bloody with a look of pain. She moved forward to get closer to him. He did not notice her. She was still too far away. That is when a dark breeze of evil blew and took Ivanka. She appeared inside a car, outside a movie theater. In the car driver seat was a woman. In the passenger seat was a man. Behind them sat Ivanka, next to a car seat. The car seat had a baby in it. The baby looked to be about six-months old. Ivanka quickly noticed the woman shrieking and screaming at the man…

The baby looked so peaceful and silent. The noise from the front of the car was muffled and almost non-existing as Ivanka focused on the features of the baby. She was a baby girl, with a cute pink bow in her light blonde hair. She was nuzzled in her car seat, carefully buckled in. The baby was tucked in with a little baby blanket. The blanket was printed with pictures of butter-flies. The color of the baby blanket was light purple. The blanket probably matched the color of her bedroom nursery walls. This baby was cute. What baby is not cute? She was especially cute, not making much noise. Not common behavior for every baby. In the eyes of this pretty baby, Ivanka saw the universe. The eyes of this baby showed that she was "thinking" – yes, this little girl would grow up to do some great things. You could sense it by just looking into her eyes. What a calm, cute baby girl – with chubby pink cheeks.The car started to accelerate forward. The screaming of the driver continued and babbling increased. Ivanka heard odd and unreasonable requests to feed the baby. The baby bottles are not made correctly, the baby is hungry, the baby is upset. And yet, there the baby girl was – still silent and calm in her car seat. The car accelerated to greater than sixty miles per hour in the parking lot and the woman increased her screams. The volume of her screams startled the baby girl. And the baby, for the first time.

Ivanka had noticed, started visibly becoming uncomfortable. This baby sensed the uneasiness in the car now and sensed violence. As the car propelled faster and faster the man in the passenger seat attempted to rationalize with the driver. Ivanka thought, you can-not rationalize with this type of person. The evil in this car was felt by Ivanka. The calm rationale talk, by the man in the passenger seat was interrupted abruptly by a quick and violent fist to the face. After the connect, the man still tried to remain calm (although it was visible that he was shocked by this violent animal like behavior). Ivanka glanced at the sad baby, then glanced back at the man as another fist connected with his face. The woman continued to accelerate the car at about seventy miles per hour, in the movie parking lot. The car was headed for some bushes, and just about 100 yards from smashing the car into the bushes….the screaming woman opened the driver's car door and jumped out of the car! The evil wind blew in and brought Ivanka to the middle of a barren desert. Ivanka was trembling with pure evil soaked fear. She had never witnessed such erratic behavior…. she had read books, horror books. But, words don't always depict the actual event. No, not unless the person is engaged in such a horrific traumatic experience will they truly understand what that could do to a person. Ivanka just hoped that the baby was okay and that the baby would not remember the violence that occurred in that car.

The Desert

Ivanka would not be "allowed" to casually stroll over to her lover, Randy. No, evil was not usually intelligent. In other words, there was no "evil head" speaking to her.

However, she was being challenged with the "winds of evil", placed into extreme, harsh conditions. She supposed that "the evil force" was doing all it could to block her from reaching Randy. And, even more concerning – the evil force in this circle of hell was guiding her to lose all sense of reality, all sense of sanity, to reach a complete breaking point. After the breaking point, the evil force would keep her in the circle of hell – away from Randy. She took a deep breath and closed her eyes. Ivanka remembered the briefings and good guidance Randy always presented to her. She trusted him. She trusted his coolness, she trusted his training, she trusted his experiences… She was connected to his heart and soul. Ivanka kept her eyes closed and sat down in the desert sand. She thought about "pillow talk" with Randy. She enjoyed his charisma, his silence and also his adventurous personality.

Ivanka recalled a conversation about training in "the harshest environments". These exercises were meant to accelerate your "state of readiness". A "prepared soldier" is half the battle. "Remember the training", and "Implement it when necessary". She opened her eyes with the "pillow talk details" in mind.

She removed her shoes and emptied any heavy items from her back pack. She kept enough water and protein bars for when she would reach Randy. And she knew that she would reach him. Love is that powerful, love is that strong. She thought of a good song, good music to hum, to sing to while she started the barefoot jog through the deserted. Her and Randy enjoyed listening to Alanis Morsette, an alternative/punk/pop style of music. They liked her music because she was certainly ahead of her time. She was innovative and part of a new genera of music called "punk rock/alternative". It really was great music and they enjoyed listening to her songs while chugging some beer, together. It was a good thing that they were both silly beer drinkers (it wouldn't be a good thing to occasionally drink if alcohol had a negative effect on a personality; some get angry...some get even worse). It was actually a funny thing to see (if anyone ever could see them). Although this behavior was all private stuff – reserved for the enjoyment of only the two of them. Sometimes, though they would get silly at some family gatherings and that was okay too (she hoped it didn't offend any family). She giggled as she jogged through the desert, thinking about how much she enjoyed listening to Alanis Morsette, and getting silly with Randy. She missed him, she couldn't imagine returning home without him.

Ivanka was a beast when it came to fitness, there was no doubt about that. However, training in harsh environments; with various military technique is a lot different than the basic jog. She was good and she knew it….so she paced herself accordingly so she would not get burnt out. Every hour to two hours she would set up a camp and rest. The edge of the desert was approaching. The evil entity still existed, but was weakened. At the end of the desert was nothing. A dead end. She sat, confused and trapped in another circle of hell. Ivanka opened her back pack, and started reading from the prayer book. Prayers offered a path to serenity, to peace. The prayers eased her mind. At the end of about twenty minutes of prayers she noticed a vision that appeared. The vision was of a family sitting in a living room home. Listening to the conversations, she recognized that the family lived in Patchogue, Long

Island. The father of the family smirked with evil happiness as his son was recently hospitalized for unknown reasons. She listened more to the weakened son entering the home, after leaving the hospital. The father, still smirking, laughed and commented on "bad coffee at the son's apartment". The coffee, it had been poisoned, no? continuing to smirk. The circle of hell on Long Island was linked with the circle of hell deep, underneath this mountain. Reflections of the evil that existed were becoming clearer to Ivanka. The network consisted of families (so-called families) that existed within the Long Island neighborhoods. The network of evil had been operating for many decades (most likely even longer than that). The network consisted of murderers, attempted murderers, and people who just knew of the crimes. And just knowing, well that made the entire community associated with the crimes. Ivanka sat on a jury one time, long ago.

And at the end of the deliberations…. the person on trial could not be proved as committing the crime. However, the person could be proved driving an escape vehicle for another known criminal during the time of the committed crime. This made this person an "associate to the crime". And under the law, the associated individual was just as guilty as if he were there, committing the actual crime. So, the vision Ivanka was seeing was a sad one (soulless women using sex as a weapon, murders being justified in their sick and twisted abnormal psyche). It was a community network that enabled crime to continue, murders to continue. The community knew of the murders, and they were associated with it. Another vision appeared to Ivanka as the elderly father visited his corrupt doctor to get a false diagnosis of "dementia". This was an added tool for the criminal associates. A tool to be used during questioning within the law. Just say "you have dementia". And this criminal got off scot free! At least on the planet earth. After this life, the souls of these people (if they had any soul remaining) would go straight to hell. Ivanka hoped that there could be some divine intervention to help save some of these associates of the devil. But to many good souls had been lost over the many decades of crime, in the communities of Long Island. The Long Island community enabled and agreed with prostitution, agreed with drug use, agreed with literally using a male body for only one purpose: to start a family, hide behind the "family", then murder the husband to collect large amounts of insurance money. These soulless women and soulless men were manipulative, seductive, very good at what they did…. and they knew they could get away with it. These criminals had roots deep in New York State agencies (the child support agency, the family court system, the child protective system, the police departments, the schools, the day care centers, the dental offices, the doctors offices, the hospitals, and more…..). This soulless "community" was pure evil. Ivanka continued to say prayers, and noticed that her blue crystal necklace was glowing. She stood up and continued to walk past the evil… the desert ended and she kept walking with hope that she would reconnect with her love, Randy. And in the closer distance, there he was! There was a clear circle surrounding him, it was surrounded with molten hot lava. The area was dark and evil. Randy stood up and sprinted toward what looked like a mid-evil stone gate (an exit). As he ran hard toward this exit, a pack of small dogs appeared. These were not the cute, small dogs you would find in a suburban Long Island home. No, these little creatures were an extension of the evil that surrounded this area. They were ratty looking, red eyed, with large sharp teeth. Jaws that were powerful, able to cling to human flesh and drag bodies back into any circle of hell. And that was what they kept doing to Randy. Every time he tried to leave the circle, and sprint to the stone gate… this pack of evil creatures appeared, snapping against the flesh on his ankles and legs. The blood was evident to Ivanka, it was dripping down his legs. Raw flesh was observed from trying multiple times to leave this circle of hell. The sharp teethed creatures dragged him back to where he started. Then would disappear.

Ivanka remembered the holy water and her golden cross. However, it was the necklace with heavenly light trapped inside that glowed intensely. More glow then she had ever seen before. It was truly amazing. The glow was a crystal bright blue and extended into an all immense globe around her body. She accelerated forward, toward Randy. The blue glowing globe protected Ivanka as she gently and slowly floated over the hellish, hot lava. She entered the stone gate and connected with Randy. The globe grew and surrounded both Ivanka and Randy. The beastly evil creatures appeared. But the evil was no match for this heavenly light. The evil creatures could not see into the globe that contained Ivanka and Randy. For now, they were safe and secure within the heavenly globe. Ivanka teared as Randy looked at her in disbelief, thinking that this may be a trick by the "evil circle of hell". One kiss from Ivanka's soft lips changed his thought though. It was her, and he said: "isn't the roth regatta boat race next week?, giggling as the shy guy she knew". She smiled and laughed. We are in a circle of hell here! And you want to know if we are ready for the University regatta boat race! Cute! She removed Randy's dog tags from her neck and placed them around his. He smiled and said: thank you, these are the shiniest tags I have ever seen! She smiled and said: "I cleaned them with your Irish spring soap". The back pack Ivanka brought contained the essentials for survival. She had Randy drink the water first. He needed nourishment. He looked like a wilted flower. He needed water and protein. The essential building blocks of life. As he was ingesting the nutrients, she reminded him of the good information they learned at University. I know, always thinking… you know that we are safe for now in this globe – and I am thankful. I am also thankful for the protein that will nurture you. All processes in the human body are connected through specialized pathways. These pathways are directed with basic building blocks: amino acids. The amino acids form chains and are called proteins. Everything in us is a protein! From our enzymes that keep us in balance, to our immunoglobulins, that protect us from invading microbes/viruses… Without the building blocks of these processes (the proteins), we cease to exist…The human body shuts down, turns off, dies without a source of protein. Ivanka didn't think Randy would have lasted much longer in this circle of hell. After the "shut down of Randy's protein regulated biological processes", the evil circle would have consumed his good soul. There was no great battle in this circle of hell. The mission was one of recon., to find her love and get him back home, with her, together. After Randy was nourished, Ivanka showed him her heavenly tools. The bible and the glowing necklace guided her all this way, to him. These tools would guide them back to the portal. They left the circle of hell with little resistance from the evil. The evil entity could not see them as they traveled in the blue sphere. Evil can truly be evil, but is mostly just a very unintelligent force. Any intelligence that may be collected by evil, is solely from the human. And this was sad, because most people are good. And any good that turns to the evil, has given up. Given up on all the good that life has to offer.

Ivanka and Randy were back at University in her dorm room. They showered together and she was soft and caring, as she cleaned his wounds. Later they rested in her bed. Ivanka and Randy were together and they were happy. Words cannot describe the level of happiness that existed. The actions of their love that followed best described their feelings. She kissed him, she kissed him in every place possible that a person could be kissed. She was soft, gentle and passionate. After he had been kissed all over his entire body…. Randy kissed her in every place one could be kissed. He was soft, gentle and passionate. They fell asleep together, in each-others embrace.

The Boat Race

They woke, refreshed from a secured night sleep together. What an amazing feeling to wake to your soul mates kiss. To wake in the morning to the warm snuggling body of your soul-mate. Words don't really describe the true feeling that is radiated…. They showered and dressed, eager to get over to the physics building. At the building where the transporter was located, they observed a large sign. The area had been "closed until further notice". They asked around in the department. Apparently, the lead (Michael) and his assistant had "disappeared". Randy and Ivanka believed that these two shitheads were soulless and returned to where they were created: the dark circle of hell, underneath the evil mountain. Ivanka did not need verification though. Not seeing them was good enough for her and Randy. They also suspected that many other "people/bodies" of evil had simply returned to the depths of hell. The real concern though was "what evil remnants had remained" in suburbia, Long Island. And they would investigate that in the near future, suspecting that more battles were imminent. However, for the time being – it was a return to University life. They were to complete the building of "card board boats", to race in the spring Roth Rigatta. This was a lot of fun, which helped break up the intense academic challenges. Randy scheduled time with his student Veterans team to help build their boat, later in the week. Ivanka did the same, for her athletic club. During the week, classes at University were far from simple. Or perhaps it would be accurate to say the it was simply: "exhausting". To listen to such technical concepts – tough stuff even for the best. Although Randy always looked at Ivanka's brilliance and wondered if this girl ever struggled to understand such difficult concepts in science (genetics, anatomy, physiology, cell signaling, evolution, chordate zoology, physics, inorganic chemistry, organic chemistry, etc.).

It was mid-week and Randy was getting to the exhaustion level that required a "power nap". This was just a strategy, a good one to survive. Some used caffeine pills, others drank lots of coffee, etc. Randy typically made his way to a student lounge where there were some empty couches. Ivanka knew he would be there, looking to place his back pack on one end of the couch. The back pack was used as a pillow. He had a few hours until the next class. And he was going to use it to take a nap. Long days sometimes, almost 12 hours in some cases – with all the things that needed to be completed. He arrived and there she was, hiding. She observed him lying on the couch on his uncomfortable back pack. She walked up to him and gently replaced the back pack with her lap. He opened his sleepy eyes and saw her. Randy smiled, then nuzzled his face into her inner thigh. Randy gently fell back asleep. She brushed his hair with her hands, softly with care….

The time during the week went by pretty fast. Both Ivanka and Randy were busy with classes. Toward the end of the week they planned to meet up, to walk over to the boat race, together. Randy was finishing a shift in the University Veterans Affairs office, where he worked part time for some cash during the semester. Ivanka was in the biological sciences building working on a marine research experiment.

Apparently, some ships from Asia inadvertently introduced a non-indigenous species of Asian crab into the Long Island Sound. The species of crab was called "hemigrapsus senguinius" (or something like that….). Her group was studying the aggressiveness of the species, by using different food. The food was placed into the Asian crab's underwater habitat, in front of a small cave. Prior to adding the food portions, the pieces were weighed. After various times, the food was removed and re-weighed. Different crab species were evaluated to determine which would go after the food, the quickest – one measure of aggressiveness. Performing the Experiment was only one area of the research. It was the library study that was the most labor-intensive part. The actual experiment was also demanding, requiring meticulous documentation and evaluation of results. She finished her section of the experiment, then headed over to the Veteran's office. They met, then left the building together. As Ivanka and Randy walked out of the building, they were confronted by a "war protest march". A group of activist students were protesting wars around the world. They were shouting and holding up signs in defiance of war. Randy walked right into the middle of this group. He felt "offended". There was really so much these protestors did not know or just did not understand. Freedom is not free. Freedom is not free. He repeated that a few times, took a good deep breath – then kept walking with Ivanka.

Ivanka always had a keen perspective on the intricacies of complicated situations. Her take on it was that this was a good environment to learn. To grow and explore. Even if it meant that some explore defiance of war… it was their opinion and right to express it. Randy smiled at her. Let's get over to the boat race. And they were there, at a nice sized lake on campus. The spring breeze blew across the lake and the fresh air felt good. The campus was alive with spirit. The boat race would commence with twenty or so different organizations (sororities, fraternities, sports groups, the student vet group, the mathematics group, the physics group and the engineering departments, etc.). The card board boat, made only of paper/cardboard and held together with duct tape were ready to race. The teams helped one or two students onto the top of each boat, and into each boat (depending on the design of the boat). Paddles were allowed. The race started and the boats raced from one end of the pond/lake, to the other end – where a finish line was decorated. Randy and Ivanka were neck in neck. Randy was paddling, but about half way noticed that the boat was soaked with water…. it was taking on and absorbing to much lake water! The boat started listing/tilting to the side and Randy went under – sinking into the fresh water. Ivanka completed the race. Of course, it was the engineering and physics departments that won first/second places in the "big University roth rigatta race". The winners were awarded a wooden boat oar (with a small gold plate: printed with "roth rigatta, and the year").

The couple was back together, excited with adrenaline! What a cool way to blow off some steam and just have fun. It broke the monotony of intense competition and grueling studies to understand and learn in this place…. What was even more fun though, was yet to come….. it was time to head over to the live bands and strawberry festival. First, they needed to shower, dry, squeeze in some loving, then they could enjoy the festival. And it was a cool spring festival. There were bands playing the latest type of innovative style music they loved. Songs by Alanis Morsette, Sum 41, Nirvana and other alternative type styles….the University landscape was fascinating…. plenty of space to nurture exploration and learning. The open land in front of the main campus library was set with the music, the bands – guitars, drums, speakers….and across from the music was "everything strawberry". Strawberry daquiris, strawberry short cake, chocolate covered strawberries, ice cream with strawberries. Strawberries everywhere…..hence, "the strawberry festival"!

The strawberry daquiris were tasty, covered with wiped cream. There was just one thing missing: vodka. The campus, what was called "a dry campus" – and it was, for most of the time (sort of). Exceptfor an occasional beer barrel or a bottle of vodka. Ivanka pulled a bottle of vodka out of her school bag. The vodka was added to the strawberry daiquiris. And it was good! Randy wasn't much of a vodka drinker, he was a sailor with a taste for rum! The vodka had a good taste in the daiquiri, and Ivanka with her Russian friends recommended It. (He thought, the vodka must be a Russian thing, then smiled).

It was early May, approaching the end of the spring semester at the University. The weather was nice. The trees and flowers had bloomed. The maintenance of the landscape was incredible. The University took good care of the landscape. Buildings were always being updated and trees, shrubs and flowers were always being planted. The colors were spectacular. In fact, some of the engineering architecture of the buildings were designed to mimic similar buildings from the state of Arizona. Why? In the state of Arizona, it was beneficial to have buildings designed to "speed up and direct wind/breezes". This was nice to have, especially in the warm, dry Arizona climate. Well, at the University in Stony Brook there was one particular building that did just that. It was pretty awesome and the breezes felt great on a warm spring day. Although, during cold winter days the breeze wasn't appreciated too much. And since Randy liked to typically wear a ball cap on his head – during the windy walks, the cap would blow off… which was somewhat annoying at times. But, other than that – the design of campus buildings, with colorful landscapes added to the learning experience. Randy supposed that it helped with the "reflection" and "pondering" of difficult concepts, theories….and their application to practical situations.

College was different than the "high school experience". Especially at the University. At University, it was intimidating at times, overwhelming at times. Randy learned to "prepare". To prepare meant to invest an incredible multi-dimensional strategy. The strategy was similar to military approaches. So, he thought why not apply the military approaches to the learning experience. It helped him. One approach was not always the only way though. But the University student needed to have some sort of strategy to learn. And there was no way around the reading, writing, studying, studying, studying, studying, applying concepts, attending resource rooms for extra help with geeky teaching assistants, and any other method that would add to the strategy. The high school year typically ended by late June in the north east region of Long Island. In college, there was four months of intense work - that always came to a cumulative crash by early to mid-May. Then it was over until late august, unless a student decided to enroll in some summer classes. Randy was in a lecture hall, early morning with his egg sandwich. He liked tograb an egg sandwich at the campus deli before heading to physics lecture. He knew he didn't have to attend every lecture. No one cared to take attendance. Why? The attendance was for your benefit. That was one of the parts to an effective learning strategy. Attend most of the lectures, take lots of notes. Then spend ample time re-writing notes, high lighting notes, trying to understand what in the world the professors meant.... cross referencing with countless days of reading textbooks, etc. In the lecture hall, the seats were ample. The hall could hold 1000 plus students. And the hall did just that at the beginning of each semester. But, like most difficult science and math courses at the University – by semesters end there were only a few hundred students that remained. Or one could say, the students that "survived".

There were plenty of seats in the main part of the orchestra style stadium lecture hall. Randy enjoyed leaving the main part of this lecture hall to grab a seat in the "balcony section". It was private, away from the technical stuff, but close enough to still hear the professor. He wasn't that guy who sat at the front of the class, raising hands to add minutes to lecture. Its not that he was never like that. Its just that with some of these tough courses, most did not know exactly what the professor was driving at in the beginning. The concepts were tough, required many nights of study to get a handle on all of it….to fully understand how it worked…. Sitting in the top balcony section, alone eating his egg sandwich – Randy was greeted by Ivanka. She sat next to him, very close to him. Lecture was still in session, and Randy re-directed his attention on Ivanka's glossy pink lips. What is that you are wearing on your lips? She giggled… wouldn't you like to find out! She had a new shiny lip gloss on and it had blueberry flavor. That lecture was the best physics lecture Randy ever sat in. Afterward, she nuzzled her cute head in Randy's neck/ chest region. Lecture ended, the students spilled out of the lecture hall. Randy and Ivanka took a nap together, in total bliss. It was Heaven on Earth. "Heaven on Earth" is possible when you are with an angel.

They woke, together. Smiled at one another then started talking about the evil that still existed in the Patchogue Medford area/surrounding areas of Long Island. Ivanka made a point about what she had seen during her trip to rescue Randy. The visions of evil. Some of the people, where they lived, where they worked… She asked Randy what he thought they should do about it. Randy looked concerned and rightly so, since one of the visions showed his own family members. He pondered a bit, then closed his eyes. Let's finish this semester strong. You plan to continue renting your room in that house near University? She said "yes lover". Good, we know where we will be sleeping this summer. She said: "as long as we are together, that is all that matters…". He took a breath, smiled at her and asked her if she wanted to take a ride with him. To where? Randy had been ordered to perform training in the pacific, an island called "Hawaii". She jumped up, out of her seat… Hawaii! she said: Yes, Yes !

Randy explained that it wasn't going to be all fun for him. Pretty tough stuff and at times very challenging in the heat… but for Ivanka, well – Randy smiled and said "you are going to like it". Randy had asked permission for her to come along with the team. The commander approved his request. She was so excited. Randy needed to brief her… for the travel. He advised that he had already been working on this for some time….and wanted to surprise her. He hoped she didn't mind that he had submitted a "special government form eighty six", to obtain a temporary top secret clearance. She smiled, hugged him, then pressed her blueberry flavored lips on his lips. Yea, that physics lecture was the best lecture he would ever remember at

University… for sure, and it wasn't because of the deli egg sandwich!

Hawaii

The semester came to an end. It was mid-May when Ivanka moved into an apartment, near The University. Randy and Ivanka spent a lot of time together. After all, that is what couples do when they truly love each other. Time apart is okay. Some time… they say absence makes the heart grow fonder… Randy supposed there was some truth to that. But, tell that to the soldier receiving his "dear john letter", after being apart from his sweet heart for a short four-month mission. Absence was a good test of true intentions, he thought. Ivanka and Randy were packed for a two-week mission to Hawaii, in June. The trip to the Pennsylvania military air field was about five hours. They drove to the base during the day. Upon arrival, they were stopped by armed guards at the secluded front gate. Randy presented two military identification cards. Each card had a computer chip in it, containing the entire life of both Randy and Ivanka. The cards were verified, the vehicle was checked. After identification, the official copy of orders was presented. The guards gestured them to move forward, onto the base. Ivanka was curious about the verification process. Randy advised that the base "did not exist", the mission "never happened" and you are to be discrete for fifty years (gag order). She smirked in her cute way. President John Kennedy said to not ask what your country can do for you…. ask what you can do for your country! Randy smiled back at Ivanka, looked into her eyes and said: don't worry, your complete record is filed away in D.C. and if uncle Sam needs you, you will be contacted. They giggled, but in a serious way. God only knew what the future held for a great nation. Preparation was a good place to start. "being mission ready" was always the goal.

They arrived at a small building, parked the car then observed a huge plane. The plane was similar to a C30 transport model, only a lot larger. This bird looked aerodynamic, with a strange black metallic shine. Ivanka knew her physics, and the design of this aircraft seemed to defy modern mathematical formulas. Randy turned to her, let's meet the team then board the plane. He introduced Ivanka as the engineer expert, who was here to help with a part of the mission. The commander (Roberts) shook her hand and welcomed her aboard the plane. The interior of the aircraft was not a nice commercial style with multiple seats. No, there was space for military vehicles, military floating crafts and a few bucket seats on the interior side walls.

The plane took off gracefully, with such a slow but deliberate effort. They seemed to hover in the air,

only inches from the ground for ever. Then, very slowly the large plane gained altitude. It was amazing that such an aircraft could even get into the air. Once in the air though, the flight across the United States moved pretty quick. During pacific-ocean travel, the plane climbed to an incredible altitude that defied modern physics. In fact, the plane was able to reach a place in the atmosphere that bordered outer space. And that is when the top inner ceiling changed from a solid opaque color to a clear/translucent see-through material. It was truly spectacular to Ivanka….she did not believe that this was possible. Flying across the pacific-ocean was a memorable experience. Together, they watched the calm, peaceful scenery.The plane touched down at Hickam Air Force base, Hawaii. The main island was home to "Pearl Harbor". Across the street from the memorial was "Aloha Football Stadium". Randy had a rent-a-car ready for him and Ivanka. They said their good byes to the team and started travel on Highway 1. There were only two main highways on this main island. Ivanka and Randy were heading to a hotel on the sandy beach of Waikiki. The island was amazing. The tropical environment was refreshing to these two Long Islanders. After they arrived and checked into the hotel, they walked together on Waikiki beach. It was early evening and they felt jet lagged. It wasn't to late for a refreshing drink by the water though. Such beauty in this aqua blue water! The culture was so different. Immediately apparent was the "Polynesian culture". There was also a lot of "Elvis Presley" music being played. Elvis visited Hawaii, made a few movies there (blue Hawaii) and it really left an impression! Wherever they walked they could see some photo of Elvis or hear his music.

Randy and Ivanka sat on the smooth white sandy beach of Waikiki. They watched the sun complete setting. The island was so peaceful. The sand was warm and soft. The water was crystal aqua blue. They talked about attending an island luau. Randy would be busy training most of the time, but the luaus were typically in the evening. It was great fun and entertainment that incorporated island traditions, music and food. For example, the "Poi" was available as a protein rich food, eaten typically by islanders. A pig was also roasted/cooked in the ground. Then eaten during the festivities. Randy was curious about what Ivanka had come across, before she rescued him. She talked about the evil that existed on Long Island. She had terrible visions of Randy's family. Specifically, his father, his brothers, mother and sisters. They were part of a tangled web of criminals. Most people were good on Long Island. It's just that this "evil network" had roots in the suburban community. Some of this evil, maybe more than "some", owned homes, worked in doctor's offices, hospitals…..Some of this evil also had hooks in community school districts and were fueled/enabled by NY State financial hierarchies. She believed some of the evil went all the way up to the top levels of the state, and perhaps beyond. They needed a strategy. A plan of attack against this evil. And that is what they would come up with. However, for now they just wanted to enjoy the peaceful Waikiki beach and the vodka fruit drinks. Ultimately, they drank a little too much and got silly. They were together and they were happy on the island of Hawaii.

Randy spent most of the time training. However, there were a few days that were "R and R". Rest and Relaxation. The island was filled with great tourist spots. A volcano had fallen into the pacific ocean and later became a beach. They drove up the volcano (the part that remained), and then down into the beach area. After parking, Ivanka rented snorkel gear for the beach. The sand was fine, soft and very dark ash in color. A different type of beach, compared to the beaches of Long Island. The water was crystal blue and calm, sparkling with tropical sun light. Randy was setting up the blanket on the beach while Ivanka anxiously jumped in the water. In the distance, Randy admired the angel that stood in this water. There were so many outstanding features that Randy loved. A true testament to the existence of a God. Only a God could create such a beautiful soul. She had a keen sense of fashion and a way to present that fashion, where ever she walked… or swam. In the distance she stood waste deep in the water. Her golden hair sparkled with the sun light and the mirror images reflected off the water. Her bikini was a dark red with a plaid pattern in dark green/black. It suited her well, offering one of those memorable moments in life… where a snapshot of such elegance forever lives. On a tropical island or a place that reminds one of the cool ocean breeze, the shiny sunlight on water – a pretty soul stands in a plaid bikini, forever. Randy caught Ivanka's attention, placing his hand up in the air – be there in a minute. The military swimmer has the ability to speed through water – with ferocity, might – cutting the water, similar to the grace of a dolphin swimming. As Randy sped through the ocean water he placed his hands on the bottom of the ocean floor, surfaced for a brief gasp of air...then went under as he continued to swim toward Ivanka. They met each other in Hanauma beach water (the name of the beach), hugged, kissed....then, they just stood there in silence. No words were needed. The silence and the beauty of this heavenly soul was eternal...Randy could have stood there the rest of the day, in silence and be the happiest man on Earth. They placed the funny snorkel gear on and swam further into the Pacific. The tropical fish were amazing. They swam with their heads partially submerged, while they breathed through a snorkel tube. The fish were colorful and friendly. As they had their heads submerged in the water a huge wave came crashing at them. They were disoriented and Randy stuck his leg in a sharp coral hole. The coral was absolutely beautiful, but very hard and sharp. Who knew what was lurking in the hole? Randy reacted quickly to get his leg out of the coral hole. As his leg came out of the hole, he scraped his skin against the sharp coral. The wound immediately started to bleed into the surrounding ocean water. Did you see where the hell that wave came from? Well, we are far into the Pacific ocean….waves like that happen all the time… Ivanka laughed.

They continued to snorkel and enjoy the scenery. Randy didn't think much about the blood from his wound. As they snorkeled, Randy felt like someone or something was watching him. Sort of a sixth sense feeling. And he was right. A shark (not to big, but big enough to give a good bite) was following him! As he turned his head in the water, through the goggles he came face to face with this beast. It was brief, and the shark was scared off (surprisingly). Ivanka and Randy swam back to the shore and were discussing what wildlife could be out in the depth of this ocean area. Just then, people on the beach were frantically discussing the presence of sharks! They looked at each other, smiled and said "okay, no more snorkeling, let's go to the luau…". The luau was awesome, full of island traditions. The music of course had Elvis Blue Hawaii, and other great tunes. The food was good and there was always plenty of fresh pineapples. The pineapples from Hawaii were the sweetest they had ever or will ever taste. These indigenous pineapples were certainly special to the island. Randy supposed that the coconuts were special to, but there was something about the pineapples. Sweet and fresh were two words that came to mind. At the hotel there was a man-made lake. The next day was rainy, but tropical. Ivanka brought Randy through a wooded area that led to a boat launch. They sat there, in the rain. There was something romantic about the scenery – the rain, the tropical air, sitting on the boat launch... She climbed on top of Randy's lap, fully clothed.

They just kissed and hugged for a good half hour....it was nice. Randy and Ivanka knew that the nice time on this pretty tropical island was coming to an end. They would head back to the circle of hell soon.The suburban areas of Long Island were wonderful, for many good souls. Souls that enjoyed the beaches, worked hard and lived, laughed and loved. Randy suspected that the circle of hell existed for many decades, and was a result of co-existence with true criminals. True criminals "bullied" some good people of the suburban areas. And over time, some good people turned "evil". They turned to a dark side due to fear. Sadly though, a good person that allows evil to exist – is enabling evil. And is thus evil. These people were enablers of crime, all kinds of crime. From simple crime to the most despicable level of crime; murder. So, even if these "good people" in the community did not commit the crimes, they were in fact enabling criminals to thrive.

The angel that visited Ivanka, had provided her with visions of the evil. The angel advised that too many good souls were lost over the many decades of evil. Too many "shows" were being played that were a complete falsification of the truth. It was pure evil. Lives were destroyed by these evil people and it was time for it to come to an end. The ring leaders of the evil force in suburbia was a school custodian and a school guidance counselor. Through these two shit heads the flow of evil circled and thrived. The community followed, due to sheer fear of what these characters were capable of. They were capable of orchestrating "accidents", "murders", "sickness", "financial devastation", etc.

Back in the Circle of Hell: Long Island, Suburbia

Long Island school districts were considered "good schools", by Long Islanders. Perhaps they were, perhaps they had an inflated ego? Randy had a friend of the family that was a professor at a local college. He remembered this family friend speaking sadly about some of the high school teachers. Specifically, high school teachers that earned a few extra bucks as adjunct professors – at night. He was sad because these high school teachers could not differentiate "high school" from "college". It was a strong "ego" that existed. The "high school teacher ego" was so counter-productive to "college curriculum". In college, the curriculum is there as the "foundation" to the learning experience. The "process" of the learning experience took years, and was not "high school". High school was more of a "controlling" atmosphere….and some of these high school teachers brought that attitude up to the college level.

Randy's family friend was more interested in presenting the college curriculum. That was challenging enough. And with his friend's experience, he would listen to the college students and this helped guide him to re-enforce (that is spend some additional time) on some of the more difficult areas (that were difficult for a particular group of students). Each semester, there were different challenges – with different learning curves, based on the student's backgrounds…. Randy's brother worked as a guidance counselor. It broke his heart that his brother was one of the "evil" entities. The bad custodian was in the same school as his brother, and they were funneling the evil through the Long Island Communities! It had to be stopped, and with the grace of God's angels, it would be. Ivanka and Randy shared a bottle of wine, snuggled, then fell asleep together….

A Long Island School District: The Hub of Evil

The role of the teachers in the high school of every school district on Long Island was essential to the "learning experience". The teacher really could have a good impact or a "not so good impact" on each and every student. Not all students were destined for colleges, but each teacher was responsible for working as hard as they could to ensure that the students learned. The learning was a process and the surroundings in the high school nurtured the growth of every student. The United States lacked some areas of expertise in areas of science and math. This was evident when comparing the curriculum and the "time in class through-out the year". Randy had enrolled in all the basic high school sciences and mathematics classes (biology, chemistry, physics, pre-calculus, algebra, geometry and trigonometry).

This was essential to building a solid foundation. The guidance counselors were responsible for scheduling the classes for students and for "directing their learning path". Randy's guidance counselor wasn't much help. Randy had been interested in some big schools, like Princeton and Harvard. But,

SAT scores were a bad factor. The SAT score was used as a major "predictor for future performance" in academics. Randy was average in the score (perhaps, just below average). The thing was, the reading and interpretation of words were so "boring". He skimmed most of the questions and readings during the testing… looking back on this, that was probably not the best strategy for success! He had learned that in order to prepare for the SAT test, a good year or more was needed. You couldn't just study a few weeks or even a few months before. But, on Long Island – in the circle of hell, there was little guidance.

Later-on in school curriculum, Randy spent countless hours, days, months, years studying and learning. Building pragmatic experience that could be applied to real challenges. He sat for graduate exams and scored much better in academic test areas (especially the creative writing area). This was great, but not as good as brilliant Ivanka. Her aptitude for glowing brilliance was evident in the way she carried herself, the way she studied, her performance.... and Randy always admired that about her – he loved that. The role of teachers and guidance counselors was one of "good faith". Good faith, that they were always following the curriculum that was approved by the academic boards. That the student was always placed first, and the learning environment was no place for politics. No politics, at any level – not at a personal level, not at a group level, etc. The school was enriched with school spirit, dominated with talk about the big football game (a pep rally). Many groups existed and thrived in the social elements of the high school. Randy's brother enjoyed coaching football and was a big part of the social elements. That was good for the students.

There were many groups within the high school. There were the sports players (the jocks), the musically inclined (band geeks, orchestra, stage crews, the actors/actresses), the black leathered "burn outs" (as they were some-times called). This group liked to sit on the edge of the high school ground and smoke. They also enjoyed "rock and roll music", "a good party" and the "mosh pit". Another group that existed were the preps and the academically superior teams. Randy admired all of the groups. The only problem he recalled was simply with the element of "evil", which existed in any group. In fact, he thought back to his time at the school where his brother now worked. Randy was a hybrid, between the "band geek" and the "jock". He enjoyed the thrill of weight lifting in the school gym and playing a musical instrument in the wind ensemble. High school could be a "weird-time...". Actually, that was typically the case for most people – in every social elemental group. The surroundings, where learning was nurtured with school staff was essential. The school should make every effort to "enhance" the learning process. Nurture school spirit, even if there wasn't much school spirit. Then of course, a student could flip the bird at all that school spirit stuff and spend time with the "burn outs". Randy recalled admiring a cute blond, with a leather jacket. She spent some time with the "burn outs". During that time, she had introduced Randy to "rock and roll", "the cigarette", her "fish net stockings", some shared "whiskey", the "mosh pit" – and so much more. And he was eternally thankful for that place/time. The memories that Randy recalled were not to different from the lyrics found in the Bon Jovi song "Thank You For Loving Me".

Randy's brother's name was "Jimmy". He was younger than him, very athletic with intelligence. His area of expertise was "school psychology". The role of guidance counselor was an important position at the high school for Jimmy. He spent many hours interacting with high school students. Guiding them, nurturing the learning experience and preparing their schedules for upcoming school years.

The Angel's Visit

Randy and Ivanka enjoyed the summer, together in the Stony Brook area. Although the circle of evil was very much still alive. It had been weakened, with the destruction of the mountain. What remained in the Long Island community was hidden, much like a lizard blends into his environment. It was a very effective survival mechanism. The evil survived in the community, lived in the community, thrived and caused an incredible amount of devastation. These evil entities had been in the community for at least four to five generations, maybe even for a greater amount of time. The local Stony Brook Chinese/ Japanese restaurant, the "pavilion" was a favorite of Ivanka's. She would often stop there to pick up dinner for Randy and her. Even though the University was not in a full "active state" during the summer, there was still much happenings… there were summer classes and various summer programs. Randy and Ivanka enjoyed the wonderful libraries, which contained ample amounts of scientific literature, books and resources. They continued their "exploration of knowledge" at the University during the summer, on their own time. The pursuit of knowledge was not only for the sciences and not only for the passion of music.

They also enjoyed Frost and Shakespeare poetry. They read books for fun. For example: "to Kill a Mockingbird", "Call of the Wild" were Randy's favorites. And, "Frankenstein" was another great story. True academic personalities by day… and lovers by night.One summer evening, Ivanka met Randy at her apartment/room, located at the edge of the University. She brought him some bamboo shoots with spicy beef, and white rice. Dumplings were the appetizer that they shared. After dinner, they watched a movie together. Snuggled and fell asleep in each-others embrace. It was the middle of the night, when they were visited by Randy's aunt. She was a beautiful angel that had helped them, guided them through the tough challenge in the mountain. The

angel had helped them in so many
ways that they had known about, and
in so many ways that they were not
aware of - in their life.

They were gently woken by the
glowing blue/white light of this
angel. She advised them of the
two evil components/entities that
still existed in the Long Island
community. These two evil forces
were effectively directing the evil
activities, and were followed by
many other evil people (through
fear). The fear was there that if
these evil minions did not follow
the evil guidance counselor and the
evil janitor, they would be certainly
maimed or murdered. And if that did
not happen, other people in their
life would be targeted, by the evil
agendas. The angel described the
evil they were dealing with. They
were not human. The soul was not
there. No, it was more of an evil
darkness, where the soul should be.

Randy sighed as he listened to the angel. Randy remembered growing up, and recalling the excessive amount of woman his brother would womanize. Randy never understood how men/boys (which ever) could "go through/so to speak" so many women. It turned his stomach. For Randy, he could count his relationships (not many) on his one hand. And on the other hand, he would consider the few women, love encounters with deep friend ships. For Randy, he would spend much time with a woman and enjoy her company. He did not understand how a good conscience could do anything else. Perhaps, sometimes people change and it was just a phase for his brother. That could be…..for some…… but, after listening to the angel, it seemed that it was just an evil cloud that existed.

Monsters exists, monsters are real. And these two characters (the counselor and janitor) were real monsters that had an evil core/ with werewolf feature. These were not good monsters and they needed to be destroyed. When attacked, the angel advised that these monsters had super strength and would change into the beast that they were. The only way to kill each monster would be with a pure silver bullet, blessed in holy water. The janitor would be especially difficult to kill, he had been around longer and carried more evil strength. The janitor existed with deep roots in the community – always on the job, owned a house and travelled often within the suburban community, fixing shit in people's homes. During his travels, he would sleep with many unsuspecting suburban wives, infect them with his evil, then gain control of their minds. Randy and Ivanka thanked the glowing angel. They wished they could hug her with all their love. The angel smiled and stated "your love for each other was "enhanced", "bridged" and "enlightened" with my (the angels) glowing hugs." That feeling of love that Randy and Ivanka felt – was also felt by the angel. The angel thanked Ivanka and Randy for carrying on with all the good and heavenly light on this earth. It was needed and it would be tested as they approached the two evil entities, in the Patchogue-Medford community: Jimmy (the school guidance counselor) and Peter (the school janitor).It was early September, and Randy did not want to leave the bed with Ivanka. He wanted to stay snuggled in her sweet perfume, soft skin and hair for all of eternity. They fell back asleep. While sleeping Randy dreamed a dream so real...he was in the school where his brother worked. The school was starting a fresh new year. The students were walking around, looking for their classes and finding their lockers. Notebooks and some textbooks were placed in the school lockers. Randy could smell the clean, sanitized school building and the "energy" from students. He noticed two particular students: a guy named Danny and a girl named Heather. They were walking hand in hand through the school halls. They stopped at "her locker". Randy could see that they had organized a system in the locker, where she placed some of her books and he placed some of his books. They were sharing her locker. Next to the locker were two different classrooms. The conversation between these two was of an attempt to move into the same physics class. "The classes met at the same time", "the classes were both Physics", "the only difference was two different teachers". She had a tough looking teacher (he was a teacher by day and a commander in the US Navy Reserves by night). Danny's teacher was this nice lady, with a strong aptitude for science.

He liked her, she was a good teacher. It's just that he wanted to be in the same class as Heather. Danny seemed pissed that the guidance counselor would not approve the transfer.

In the dream/the vision, Randy re-focused his attention. In the close distance was an evil looking custodian. The janitor was watching Heather and Danny. The janitor, Peter, was talking to himself in the most odd way: "look at those two, hugging, French kissing – this is a public high school!", They don't know anything about "true love"…. and Peter went on a rant… I will show that shit that he can't do that in this school…..I will stage an accident, like the others….. that will take care of him. Or better yet, the Brookhaven dumps are right down the road……I can have it arranged, get his body in a hole, deep in the dumps…..its worked before, it will work again.

Randy thought, my God — this guy is a murderer….pure evil! Randy recalled a writing: "murder is like potato chips, you can't stop with just one" (paraphrased, SK). Peter, the janitor was charming at times, always on the job — and sleeping with all the married women in the suburban community. And for the people that Peter did not like, well — he murdered them or had them murdered. Randy heard this janitor ranting to himself about ways to stage "accidents", "place his dead poisoned body in a car in a busy intersection and stage a car accident… maybe add some alcohol to the vehicle, that would be a good crime scene!Randy woke in a sweat, and Ivanka held him. She could see that he was frightened and visibly upset. He told her of the dream… Randy was so sad for the community on Long Island, plagued by an evolution of good people with evil criminals. This had been going on for so long, decades upon decades had passed and things had gotten better for these evil people… things had gotten worse for the victims, the good people of the community. Randy feared for their lives. In addition to all that, the state agencies were corrupt. Child Protective Services – well they served the criminals, the soulless criminals. There were not enough laws for the children; Randy thought. He said to Ivanka: "there should be more specific laws to protect the children from psychological abuse". These criminals use the "children" as pawns in a sick and twisted psychological game. These evil entities did not care, they had no souls. Randy thought, at least if a law was approved to put these child abusers away for six months to ten years… maybe less child abuse would occur…. The laws were needed, not just at the state level, but at the federal level to. Making the psychological abuse of children a felony would help reduce the state level corruption. He thought that, anyway – he wasn't a lawyer... he was sure that a lawyer would find a way to spin all of it and in the end, it would only be the children that were hurt, mostly.

Ivanka hugged Randy and followed with the warmest and softest kiss that he ever felt on his lips, his body. She was something special. She left to take a shower. He said he wouldn't be far if she needed him, he was going to cook some bacon and eggs! She smiled and laughed... you do that lover! He thought about the breakfast, he thought about that he loved to shower with Ivanka (but, privacy was also important – he didn't want to seem like he didn't care about privacy; it was good to go study on your own sometimes, it was good to have a ladies' night out and do what ladies do – shop, dance, see a movie, whatever her heart desired…. he would always be home to keep the light on when she returned later that night……he also thought about bringing the silver bullets to the church for a blessing in holy water….).

The "Long Island Community"

The community in suburbia seemed "nice". There was lots of space, yard space for kids to run around in. Lots of space for teenagers to play the adult version of "hide and seek", "man hunt". The janitor (the evil coordinator in the community) lived in this nice suburban environment, just blocks from a huge dump. The Brookhaven dump had a devilish smell at times, which probably masked all the bodies Peter had dumped there, over the years. It had gotten to the point where it was no longer a "typical murder". No, now it was for "sport". If the janitor did not like you or if one of his minions had an issue with someone. Peter would take care of it. He would kill the son of bitch. And that was that. No real worries for "Law". The abnormal psyche of the criminal mind comforted his murderous ways. Peter knew that the courts were "civil", the courts were "forgiving". The courts were not equipped to deal with such psychosis. This janitor was not to smart, but had been around a long time. He had committed so many murders that he had gotten pretty good at it. Besides that, he had infected many good souls of married women in the community. He was also surrounded by a large group of so called "women" that truly did not have souls....they were part of the evil "network that existed". They watched the community, they informed Peter of any "waves" in normal routines. And if they didn't like someone, they would use them.... in many different ways. Use their victims, similar to a black widow spider. Then, have them killed!

Peter was tracking that son of bitch, the cool kid from his high school. The kid that loved to kiss his girl in the school halls. The kid who loved to hug. Peter was the one who visited all the "women" in this community. Peter thought, in his psychosis, that he was the one to infect the women…..not this little shit named Danny. The janitor knew that Danny and Heather were babysitting a neighbor's kid, one Friday night. He had over heard the conversation in the halls at school. Peter would be there to take care of this situation. It was a late Friday evening, and Danny met Heather across the street – from her house. She lived only a few blocks from the high school. Peter was parked at the dead-end road, waiting. The kid in the house, Ray was an energetic 6-year young kid.

He loved karate. Heather was the one babysitting for a few bucks…..Danny just wanted to spend some time with her. As Danny entered the house, Ray drop kicked him with a cool karate move. Danny wrestled with the kid, laughed then "took a break". Danny made some popcorn and read Ray a kid's story. Heather smiled…. Ray was eating so much popcorn that Danny had to tell him about the popcorn monster… he was joking, but the kid took it serious. When Danny said he would start feeling popcorn coming out of his ears if he didn't slow it down a bit……Ray grabbed his ears!

Danny kissed Heather goodnight and left the house. As he was driving down the road he was side swiped by Peter. Peter attacked Danny with a large rusty iron wrench. The body lay there, bloody. Peter was murdering for sport now. He cut off this little shit's arm, and would bury it under a slab of cement, in his backyard... next to his beautiful inground pool. As for the rest of the body... he placed it in Danny's car and moved the car to the Patchogue rail road tracks in the middle of the night. The car was hit by a passing westbound train. The local papers and news had many soulless minions that supported the "so called tragedy". Like all the other murders, there was no investigation in this Patchogue Medford community. Peter enjoyed a cool lemon aide drink at his pool during a nice autumn evening, seated on a lawn chair.... just above the buried body parts (peters bag of bones). Peter smiled and continued to drink.

"Hun-Bunny Lick"

The light in heather's eyes had changed. She was always a radiant brown eyed beauty. Her eyes shined with such brightness and zest for life. Heather was also a tough girl on the soccer field. Her athletic ability amazed Danny. Or maybe it was the combination of athletic ability with the way she appeared (to him) in the cutest soccer shorts he had ever seen on a lady. There was something about the long blond pony-tail, sparkling white checkered soccer shorts with school jersey that attracted him to her… Heather redefined the word "cuteness". She still could not believe that Danny was not in school. Her locker was filled with his notebooks and text books. He was not there to kiss her during the day, as they changed classes. After about a week, hope was dwindling. Not only was Danny missing, but other oddities were occurring around town. Increased crime, attacks and other murders. A teacher had been jogging one early morning. She was the track coach for the school. A crazy criminal attacked her, and she was sadly murdered. People in the community sensed evil. That is, the people that were "good". Most of the community, unfortunately, had a surplus of evil home owners, doctors, dentists, school staff, etc. It was a circle of evil…the good souls sensed the evil (and always lived in fear of it). Heather walked about, with such sadness, open to any evil that could easily infect her... Danny was no longer there to shield her from the evil....

The week had ended and Heather got up the nerve to visit Danny's parents house. She brought an empty school bag. She asked his mother if she could visit his room. His mother agreed, and Heather sensed some evil in the house... the mother did not seem "sad" that her son went missing. Heather walked up the stairs to the second floor of the house, alone. She continued to the furthest part of the house, where his bedroom was located. She opened the door and slowly entered. Heather loved him, she was beyond sadness. She stumbled onto the floor next to his twin sized bed and sat, as tears rolled down her face. She thought "if she could not be with him, she would take with her some important items"….She reached into his dresser and pulled out two pair of boxer shorts/underwear. Next, she grabbed two t-shirts and a red/black football jersey. She placed all this in her school bag. These items would be brought back to her house. Heather could still smell the faint scent of his "cool water cologne" and her "exclamation perfume" on his jersey. In fact, all the clothes had his scent and she loved that. She briefly had a day dream of wearing boxer shorts and the football jersey, as she slept with him – snuggled in his arms.

Heather returned home with Danny's clothes. She changed into a pair of his boxer shorts and his foot ball jersey. She lay in her bed, alone – thinking of how she missed him. She thought that she would keep these forever, as a memory of her love for him – along with the silly cassette tape he had given her (some time ago). The cassette tape had recorded music on it, that he loved to listen to… he always remarked about how creative the music was and how it was "their songs". Yeah, it was silly to her… but, not now…. the silly cassette tape became another wonderful piece that completed her heart… She teared, cried as the songs played: "Always (Bon Jovi)" and "I will always love you (Whitney Houston)". She lay there alone, without Danny. She knew that wherever Danny was, he was not sleeping well… he always loved sleeping through the night with Heather… he would thank her for loving him and always cherished the time together – true love… Heather continued to cry because she knew that he would not ever sleep well… he was that type of loyal guy… He felt complete with her love, sleeping together as her bare warm chest rested on his bare muscular pecs. She remembered him saying to her one time: "you complete me, with such a security – the security that only love offers to true soul-mates..." and Danny would sleep well through the night with Heather, because of that security. Heather felt the same way, and now... her security was missing as she tried to fall asleep. She wondered where Danny had gone, was he okay? She could feel his love through the clothes she had on......but she was alone.

The End (continued in chapter 3)

Chapter 3

At first glance, and at first
listen — you would feel empathy
for this Long Island community.
However, upon delving into the
inner workings of the community....
it became clear, sadly... that these
'people' (soulless bodies of people
with darkened souls) were bad. They
were not empathetic, they were not
capable of true love. No, the evil of
this circle of hell (and there were
certainly other hellish circles) was
plagued with an effective network of
people... that hid behind the sacred
family. That hid behind the sacred
church. That hid behind what was
supposed to be a sacred community...

with sacred schools…The evil was fueled by the top echelon of NY state, through the chambers, up into many levels of government.

The counselor (Jimmy, minion of the evil powerful custodian) had an office in the basement of the school. It was a perfect place for this evil creature. He was part flesh and part evil beast, with strength from hell. He lived a few minutes from Peter (the residential custodian, master evil entity), and the local Brookhaven dumps. A perfect landscape to commit murders. Jimmy lived in a more than modest house, in the Patchogue Medford community. In fact, the house was very big and located in a "gated community". The house had nice property in front and behind. Jimmy was married to a "wicca" practicing wife. She believed in the dark forces of nature and summoned the evil spirits during community gatherings. During these "social gatherings", a few evil couples from the gated community were invited.

The families of good souls were also invited. Heather, for example, attended some of these "parties" – and witnessed the summoning of evil witch-like spirits. The parties had much alcohol, devil's music, chants, sex, drugs and resulted in the infection of many good community residents. It was a network of evil, that continually proliferated – under the direction of a custodian and a counselor. The "parties" lasted into the late night and the "evil rituals" always resulted in tragic events. The tragedies did not occur immediately. However, the "curses" were summoned during the parties, and the tragedies occurred within a day or so after the ritual. It was pure evil. Sometimes it was an "accident" that would happen. Sometimes it was children being instructed to cross busy traffic filled roads – in hopes they would be struck by an oncoming car. Sometimes it was the addition of a little poison to cause cancer (a known carcinogen…) etc. The community thrived on the evil and lived in fear of the custodian, his wife, the school counselor and his wife.Randy woke with a gasping breath. He was together with Ivanka, in her dorm room bed. It was early autumn on the Stony Brook University Campus. She asked what was wrong? She hugged him. He told her of his dream, his vision of this guy Peter, a custodian and his brother – Jimmy. The details of the evil parties and where to locate these two evil creatures. These evil entities were part beast and part "so-called" human body. The evil needed to be destroyed and they would accomplish this with their courage, together, with the silver bullets – that they had blessed by Father Ed. It would be a journey that needed to be taken. They did not want to go, but they knew that the destruction of this evil force was necessary. It was the only thing that would save what was left of this community. They hoped that the good souls would be freed to live their lives in happiness. And as far as the soulless evil entities – these people would travel straight to hell, following Peter and Jimmy.

Ivanka was bare chested and Randy admired her beauty. It was not just what he observed in her. It was more. The light that radiated from her light blond her, the heavenly winds that emanated from her sweet perfume. Randy was a gentleman, a shy guy who was embarrassed when it came to these types of thoughts. She deserved all the modern poetry for such wonderful beauty. She hugged Randy, she could sense his thoughts – the true test of soul mates. She knew what he was thinking. Randy kissed her large light brown nipples. Very unique and pure beauty – he loved this trait in Ivanka. It wasn't the size of her breasts that turned him on, it was more of her nipples and the pheromones that were released as they made love in her dorm room bed. She could kiss, and she softly kissed him everywhere a man could be kissed and loved. He always reciprocated with more softness, gently kissing her and helping her feel his love through the sensations of his tongue. They loved each other. He was a shy gentleman with a gift of love that he was thankful to share with her. Some people travel through this life, never experiencing true love. He was thankful that she found a way to reach him…..and that was the power of love. Randy was thankful that Ivanka trusted him enough to share her love at that level. A pure beautiful soul….he felt her security, her comfort, that was strengthened with her love. Randy trusted Ivanka to….as much as she trusted him….

There was something about this time of year, on campus, that Ivanka and Randy appreciated. Perhaps it was the love of nature, perhaps it was the cool autumn breezes or the pretty colors from the bushes, flowers and trees. The environment on campus nurtured academic understanding and growth. Weather it be in the field of biology, physics, mathematics or any other subject… the scenery helped students learn and helped some fall deeply in love.They returned to the physics building basement. The transport project was closed and there didn't seem to be any talk about reopening it anytime soon. Ivanka spoke to Randy about figuring out a way to travel to other places, together. Maybe they could work the scientific formulas to calculate a travel path to Hawaii or South America. they smiled at each other and agreed to revisit this transporter in the near future. First, they needed to travel into the Patchogue-Medford community with a serious mission ahead of them.

The Patchogue-Medford landscape was nice. The homes were built in a suburban community, about half way onto the "Long" Island. There were many pine trees. In fact, parts of the community were called "the pines". And that is where Randy had a good friend. His friend had traveled to Florida for a few weeks. Randy and Ivanka went to the house in the pines. It was in the deep woods of his friend's house, that he had interest in. Ivanka and Randy parked their car in the driveway, then walked around the house into the back yard. The yard was immense. Deep in the woods was an old-fashioned type cabin. That is where they set up "base camp". In this cabin, they planned the attack on Jimmy. They had to do it right, right the first time… or they risked losing everything – including their lives. The night in the woods was creepy. It was a windy, dark night – until the full moon rose. In the sky they could see the bright full moon. The cabin was small, but had everything they needed. Some blankets, a bed and a small bathroom to take a shower. They talked about traveling to the school the next day, and waiting for the counselor in the basement – his office area.

Randy advised Ivanka that there were some things that she did not know about him. They did not keep secrets from each other. They did not lie to each other. True love does not do those things. If that sort of thing is built into a relationship…

well, it is certainly a recipe for disaster and eventual failure. Although, forgiveness and divine intervention has worked miracles for some relationships... Randy smiled at Ivanka, to lighten the serious air about the cabin. You know me, you know me well. You know about my "trainings", you've travelled with the "team" to Pearl Harbor.....you've nursed my wounds, you've rescued me from the depths of hell.... I am eternally in your debt, I could never begin to explain how thankful I am....so thankful, for "you", "being you". You are something, not of this earthly world....your soul reflects many places and many times, from this place and other universes. It amazes me and I admire such brilliance. In many ways, you are stronger than me...

As we approach the evil entity, Jimmy will change into the beast that he is. The thing is... he does not realize that what will come at him is another beast. You see, early on in the training – a select few (the team) was injected with "solutions". These liquid solutions embedded quite accurately and precisely into our DNA. The alteration was one of part "man" and part "soldier". No ordinary soldier, a hybrid of some sort that has the capability to unleash such uncontrolled vicious, aggression. This "tool" (as some called it), was a good strategic force – especially when fighting the darkest of evil. When you see the change, don't be alarmed. I will do what needs to be done to complete this mission. But, I need your help. At the right time, the blessed silver bullet will need to be fired at Jimmy in the area where his heart should be. This will finish what I will start.

They rested and prepared for the trip to the school basement. Where

Ivanka and Randy planned to wait. Some time passed, and Ivanka drove with Randy to the school. The basement was dark and creepy. Jimmy arrived and immediately sensed the presence of goodness in his chamber. Ivanka gasped for air as she witnessed Jimmies transformation into what seemed like part man and part beast, with sharp teeth – a snarling snout and dark powerful claws. Jimmy lunged at Randy, gashing a piece of his flesh, and throwing him across the room – with ease. Ivanka remembered the briefing, in the cabin. She reluctantly hid, with fear – but ready to do what was necessary to remove this evil from the community. Just then, as Randy had warned...she witnessed a transformation of Randy from man to some sort of beast. Not similar to Jimmy, but something that was more fierce and dark – then she ever saw before. Randy attacked Jimmy, aggressively – with the force of a thousand armies. After much fighting, the final blow was achieved....as Randy lunged into Jimmy's throat, then broke his jaw with a fierce punch. Ivanka sensed the final moment, then fired the blessed silver bullet into Jimmy's chest. A dark cloud brought Jimmy deep into the depths of hell. Randy lay on the floor, injured. Physically hurt, but more ashamed of his grotesque change. Randy never wanted Ivanka to see him like this. Randy longed for the days of innocence. The days, prior to the injections, the days prior to the training, the days where he innocently climbed the tallest trees on a breezy day and just admired the beautiful creation of "nature". Those days were long gone... as he changed back to a "gentleman", he passed out and fell into a vision of Ivanka caring for him. And she did, she was amazing. Ivanka dragged him back to the car and all the way back to University. He lay on her bed, in her dorm. She snuggled with him. Randy sensed her love and affection. This is the only thing (a heavenly miracle on earth, in a harsh world) that could effectively "save", compassionately "heal" Randy. Even though he did not have the days of innocence, a time that he longed to go back to. He did have Ivanka's love and affection. And that healed him, where he could smile and always be happy.

Time was needed. The time was needed to heal the wounds inflicted by battle. Eventually, they would have to go back and finish with a "final battle", which would completely free the community from the hellish cloud. The semester went by fast, and December snow fell. The campus displayed a warm glow of lights in the evening as Randy and Ivanka walked to their lab. The lab topic was "dissection of a sheep heart". It was a good lab and it helped them understand the in-depth meaning of the human circulatory system. Together, they followed instructions to dissect the heart. They observed the interior chambers and immediately noticed that there were four different "chambers". The top two chambers were called "atria" and the bottom two chambers were "ventricles". Ivanka pointed with the dissecting tools, showing Randy the immense musculature of the large left ventricle. It made sense to them as they observed the very large muscular wall. The "oxygenated blood" flowed abruptly from the left ventricle with an extreme force. It had to be propelled this way to get through the human body and sustain "life". In order to propel this life-giving oxygen rich blood from the left heart ventricle, a strong thick muscle was needed. Observing this thick muscular wall helped the students better understand the human circulatory system.

After lab, they washed with plenty of soap then walked over to the astronomy building. On the way, they stopped to get two cups of coffee. It was getting late, but not too late to enjoy some caffeine and take the elevator up to the top of the astronomy science building. At the top of the building was an "outer space observatory". Public and students gathered some nights to look through a high powered telescope, into outer space. This night was quiet, the observatory was closed – no public viewings. Ivanka pulled a soft blanket from her school bag to place on the top roof floor. Randy and Ivanka both put the coffees to the side and rolled on to their backs. The view of the night sky was amazing. As they looked long enough… they began to see "shooting stars", and "satellites". It was so peaceful, they enjoyed each other's company.

The Custodian's Next Victim

The custodian was planning his next attack. Usually, it was just easier to have one of his minion goons to carry out the attack. But this one was personal. He wanted to personally visit this 70 year old man, who worked as a part time security guard. The overnight shift was a perfect time to carry out the murder, or "accident" as the psychopathic janitor thought. Traveling to the site where the security guard was, the janitor was in a NY state of mind. He enjoyed listening to 1960s music in his truck. As he snapped his fingers to the guitar solos on the radio, he arrived. In the distance he saw his victim sitting in the security vehicle. It was 2 in the early morning. The Janitor, Peter, quickly went over to a large building that had a long deep stair case, outside. The cement stair case led down, into the building's basement. There was at least thirty large cement steps. Peter placed some "sharp stones" in the area, on the ground in front of the stair case. He also knocked out the lighting. The next part of his plan was to wait for the security guard to reach the "check point". A check point is a "station" that was checked hourly by the guard. A key needed to be scanned electronically at the station. This monitored the hourly rounds of the guard and was added to nightly security reports. A good document to have if an insurance claim needed to be processed. As the security guard approached the dark top step area, he tripped on the jagged stones and plummeted violently over about twenty hard cement steps. His ribs were cracked, broken… the impact of the human spinal column bones (vertebrae) on hard cement does not usually end well. Vertebrae were snapped, bones were cracked and broken. The security guard crawled the remaining ten steps, downward in extreme pain – spitting up blood… then passed out. Peter smiled and walked down the steps. This was more than murder… it was sport. With a sharpened hatchet, and one clean violent swing… Peter removed the security guards leg. He placed the severed leg in the back of his pick up truck and drove back to his home. As he drove, he wondered if he would place the leg under the pool shed or under the pool walkway… sipping on a cool refreshing drink….

Ivanka and Randy left the University, early the next morning. They approached Peter's home in the Patchogue-Medford community.

Around back, Peter stood sipping a refreshing lemonade drink. Randy, Ivanka and Peter met, it was "the devils meeting". Peter stood on top of "his bag of bones", smiling, sipping. Peter cackled and laughed with extra volume. Randy was about to transform into the viscous beast to finish what was started….and as Randy stood in front of Peter… the custodian continued to laugh. Just then, a brightness appeared around Ivanka. She glowed with a heavenly yellow, with the power of 1000 angelic suns. Ivanka seemingly floated toward peter and somehow, pushed Randy to the other side of the yard. She stared at Peter with such sadness… She saw through his ways of hiding behind all that was good in this world. Peter was manipulative, Peter was psychotic – a high functioning psychopath, Peter was pure evil – a murderer. As the light from Ivanka grew brighter, all the spirits from Peter's victims appeared to add to Ivanka's heavenly strength. Peter continued to laugh, even as the light of the heavens simply entered where his soul should have been... and just like that, it was over.

Ivanka and Randy returned to University. They finished the fall semester. Ivanka and Randy would spend the winter break together, getting ahead on the studies – spending time in the University libraries and in the labs…..But, first they needed to re-visit the

Physics building basement. The transport module was still there. Randy tapped Ivanka on her shoulder. He said "do you know how brilliant you are?" I mean, your "way", how you present yourself…. Ivanka giggled, smiled then continued with transport calculations. She gently brushed her sun beamed blond hair from her pretty eyes and smiled again at Randy…..He continued with the much deserved compliments. Some just admire your brilliance, some hate you for it, some are jealous, some intimidated….me, I admire everything that you are and everything that you are not. But most importantly, I "love" that you are incredibly brilliant with heavenly light brown eyes. Randy asked Ivanka: "where are we headed?" She smiled, giggled – "did you pack the bathing suits?" He did, she had asked him to before they left the dorm… Ivanka embraced Randy with a soft cute hug… they were together and they traveled through the transport module, back to Pearl Harbor Hawaii….

The End.

Printed in the United States
by Baker & Taylor Publisher Services